A PLAY ON THE WEST

SERIES: BOOK ONE

BY J. WESLEY

A PLAY ON THE WEST
SERIES: BOOK ONE

DEDICATION

This book is dedicated to the memory of my father.
Daddy, you gave us all our sense of humor.
We love you.

I wish to thank the great and patient people who
contributed to this book including:
Kelley, William, Richard, Katherine, John, Cheryl,
Amanda, Rob, Patrice, and Tim.

CONTENTS

PROLOGUE

The sun rose over a large meadow on the north fork of Elk Horn Creek west of George Town, Kentucky. Its rays dispersed the clouds of fog lingering above the blue grass. A muscular horse in labor rolled on the ground, then she stood and walked in no particular direction. Jacobus Hendrickson saw his mare was in trouble because she kept repeating these actions several times without any result, so he shouted to his wife, "Sarah, I have to get the horse doctor quick!" He ran into the barn, threw a saddle on one of their other horses, Dutch, and galloped down a road that bordered the creek. The footing was bad, and the ride was still dark in places. Jacobus didn't care because Red and her foal could both die. After riding a little over a mile, he arrived at the front door of Milton's house and yelled, "Dr. Milton – Dr. Milton!"

"Doctor" Milton or Milton Harris was an experienced horseman, farrier and blacksmith, but he was still the closest thing this entire area had to a real veterinarian. He recognized Jacobus' voice and came to the door. "What's wrong?"

"It's Red! She's in trouble with the foal! Please come quickly!"

Milton grabbed his bag and a thin rope, saddled his horse, and both men rode as fast as they could. They reached the house and ran to the pasture behind it. Jacobus heard the other horses in the barn neighing and bumping against their wooden stalls.

Sarah cried, "She's going to die!"

Milton ran to the mare and quickly palpated her – felt the foal and shouted, "It's turned – It's turned! Get me the rope!"

Jacobus grabbed the rope and threw it. Milton reached his hands inside Red and placed the rope carefully around the foal, as he had done before in these situations and carefully pulled it until the new colt was on the ground. Her heavy breathing slowed and it looked like she would be all right.

Milton, Sarah and Jacobus looked at the dark, gawky colt on the ground. Steam came off him because the ground and the air were cold and damp, but no one cared about the weather. They all watched the colt stand up and take his first steps. Sarah wiped tears from her eyes as she hugged Jacobus and Milton.

"We were lucky," Milton said, "very lucky."

"Hawkeye's birth wasn't near that much trouble," Jacobus said. "We might just name his little brother Lucky after that. What a morning!"

Milton pointed at the new foal. "He looks just like Hawkeye – see that little star of white between his eyes? It's almost identical to Hawkeye's isn't it?"

Jacobus heard the horses in the barn and walked inside to calm them. Soon he reappeared and shouted, "Good lord, Milton – you were right! The spot on Hawkeye is almost the same"

"You have some special horses there, Jacobus."

In the months that followed, Lucky grew from a young colt to a strong yearling. Most of the neighbors who saw Lucky during this time called him "Little Hawkeye." They always remarked that, "The only difference between those two horses was time."

As Lucky grew, he and Hawkeye became inseparable.

They always ran after each other in the creek pasture. For a year, Jacobus saw Hawkeye was the faster horse and acted like he knew it. He always taunted Lucky into chasing him and once Lucky closed the distance, Hawkeye turned on his real speed and left Lucky far behind. They played like this for months.

This spring, however, was different. The rains were much heavier in March and April. One day, Hawkeye and Lucky ran in and out of rising water on the creek pasture, but now Lucky was almost catching him. Hawkeye wanted to test Lucky to see if he could really keep up, so he turned away from the creek bank and bounded into the rising water. Hawkeye looked back to see that Lucky stopped. Hawkeye moved his head up and down grunted loudly in triumph and then stepped in an area where the water was much too deep. He couldn't feel the river bank with his hoofs and tried to swim back, but the current was too strong and swept him away. Lucky could still see Hawkeyes' head, so he quickly ran to another part of the pasture to get a better view, but when he got there, Hawkeye was gone.

CHAPTER ONE
THE DREAMER

An angry voice reverberated throughout a large mansion off Main Street. "Riley! What are the damned lawyers doing now?"

The accountant, Riley Draggart, frowned and climbed the steep staircase again. When he was a few steps from the next floor, he became eye level with a white and black spotted rat terrier named Spivey cowering on the floor under a large wooden desk. After he reached the top of the staircase, he saw his muscle-bound, scar-faced boss leaning back in a chair with his feet on the desk, and asked, "Is it the McConnell property again?"

Anton Greeley threw the folder he was reviewing onto the desk. "That's just it. It's *not* the McConnell property!"

"Anton, they have simply been keeping you updated on their chain of title work. Sage's firm has been looking at all the prior owners and surveys in Scott County and George Town itself. When we think we have a case for you, we sometimes use your other corporations to sue so the whole town doesn't *quite* know the reach of *Anton Greeley*."

"You're starting to sound just like them Riley. You're all stuck in the mud. All this lawyer crap takes too much time!"

"Anton, the titles go back a long time. We've got to have the proper challenge in court or it's all for nothing. Remember why we left Philadelphia – *Fist*?"

"Not funny Riley. I know we can't force everyone to do things, but we're going to grow old at this pace."

"I thought the *Fist of Philly* days were over because you didn't want the law all over you."

Greeley placed his feet on the floor, sat forward in his chair and pounded his right hand on the desk. "I'm not boxing anymore, and I haven't beat down anyone in a long time, but this never ends. The only people benefiting now are the goddamned lawyers!"

"Anton, you have a huge three story mansion here, and a life that is not quite *yet* under suspicion – relax..."

Anton Greeley turned red and bolted up so fast that he knocked his chair onto the floor. Then he awkwardly grabbed a pencil off the desk and threw it at the wall behind his accountant. It hit the wall and ricocheted underneath the desk. The terrified Spivey jumped up and hit his head on a drawer and darted out from beneath the desk to the bedroom. Greeley yelled, "Bullshit! I'm not waiting forever! Do you understand what I am telling you?"

"Yes Anton."

"Good! I'm going to the Stirrup and Heel."

Riley Draggart attempted to change the tone after the outburst and meekly said, "Again? What about Pratter's Hotel Bar? It's so much closer."

"Not my kind of people Riley...bunch of showboats!" Then, without saying another word Anton Greeley grasped the handrail, slowly stepped down the steep staircase and slammed the door on his way out.

On the other side of town, a young, sassy Katherine Hinrichs stood up, held her fists at her side and piercingly asked, "Mama, why do we have to live in such a small house?"

Elizabeth Hinrichs quietly said, "Lower your voice.

Daddy's working on getting a bigger place. You need to show patience."

"Haven't you seen the houses on the other side of town? Some of them must have fifty acres!"

"They aren't fifty acres, Katherine."

"I bet some of them are!"

Elizabeth lowered her voice. "You might be right, sweetheart."

"When do we get a bigger place, Mommy?"

Her father, Joseph Hinrichs, easily heard Katherine from another room. Her question pained him because he had tried to be a successful farmer in this area, but he and Elizabeth both wanted more. He felt obligated to keep working hard and thought that maybe, someday, their time would come. The Hinrichs family were not alone.

Parts of Kentucky had become wealthy with great culture. Most residents wanted to stay in this thriving community, but other farmers and ranchers were dissatisfied with what they were able to earn. Will Richards had been one of the largest cattle ranchers in Scott County on a large tract of land that he worked southwest of the Hinrichs family. He was a tall strong man in his thirties with thick light brown hair. He worked hard and liked to have fun, but always set large goals for himself. Like the Hinrichs family, he wanted more *a lot more* as he thought again this day. He was always looking for another challenge. George Town, to him, was changing for the worse because more people like Greeley were arriving all the time. Richards came to view his ranching efforts in Scott County as a stepping stone. The real challenge to him with the greatest opportunity was far west of Kentucky.

Miles Harris was another cattle rancher in Scott County. He and Will became friends as children because their father's fought together in the Revolutionary War before Kentucky was a state. As the youngest children from both families, they grew up listening to many years of war stories.

That day, Will rode to meet Miles for their weekly trip to George Town. The conversation he was going to have with Miles, however, was anything but routine. As Will approached their usual place south of town on Cross Street, he saw Miles atop his light chestnut quarter horse named Chipper, but he couldn't see Miles' face – only the top of his hat. After a few more seconds, Will thought *he's asleep,* so he walked his mare, Millie, a little closer – then smiled and shouted, "Miles, wake up!"

Miles sat up in the saddle like a shot, his mouth open and his eyes wide. Chipper immediately reared up on his hind legs. Miles, still holding the reins, quickly wrapped his arms around Chipper's neck and whispered, "It's okay – it's okay" in Chipper's left ear, then gently pulled back on the reins, but after his front hooves hit the ground, Chipper began to run. Miles pulled the right rein and turned Chipper in circles before he finally calmed down. "Damn you Will! Why'd you do that?"

"You were asleep!"

"If you'd been here waiting this long on *you* and your slow horse, you'd fall asleep too!"

"I don't care how fast Millie is. She always gets me where I need to go."

"Right, like your father used to say about their horses – *so slow they lulled the enemy to sleep.*"

"No Miles, my dad said that about your dad's horse when they were fighting the British."

"No Will, *my* dad outthought the limey bastards and those Indians with his mind not his horse."

"You aren't remembering what he said, Miles. They

used diversions to make the enemy think they had more soldiers than they did. They didn't do it with fast horses."

"That's what I'm saying – but their horse raids with their swords made the difference!"

"Yeah, but only after the first few volleys! Too bad your dad's sword skills didn't rub off on you."

"What? I beat *you* this past summer at the Fourth of July burgoo, and you know it!

"You almost fell off Chipper, barely clipped that melon, and dropped your sword. They gave it to you."

"You are so full of shit, Will."

"Alright – stop. I have something important to talk to you about right now."

"What? You found another woman you like at Pratter's Hotel bar?"

"Nope – I've heard from Michel."

"Michel Germain Rocheteau. I haven't heard that name in a while. How is the fur business for him going way out west?"

Will turned to wave at one of their neighbors on the road travelling south and said, "Not good, Miles. He got out of that a long time ago – where have you been?"

Miles waved at the same neighbor and said smugly, "I haven't kept up with him like you have, Will. I *do* know he left here with his dad few years back to go into the fur business."

"Miles – just stop. You know the fur business went south a long time ago. Michel said in his letter that the land business in Mexican California, though, is *very* good."

"Good for Michel – now speaking of Pratter's, let's go there again tonight while we're in town?"

"He's bought two leagues of land, Miles."

"Two leagues! That's over eight thousand acres, Will –

way more than both of our places here combined! How'd he do that?"

"After the Mexican government took over from the Spanish in Northern California, they made it easier to purchase enormous amounts of land. Michel became a Mexican citizen, and from what he said in his letter, he's married now to a beautiful woman from Mexico."

Miles pulled on Chipper's reins because the horses had started to lower their heads to nibble grass on the roadside. "Who in the world would marry Michel?"

"You sound jealous."

"I can't believe he's still alive, the way he deliberately seeks out trouble."

"You're missing the point. What's important to us now is being able get our hands on that much land like he did. We can do it, but we need to get out there as soon as we can while the land is available."

Miles didn't reply.

"This is the opportunity we wanted, Miles. Look at the way things are now. The amount of land we have here is really limited for what we want to do."

"I know we don't have the biggest operations, Will – but California?"

"Yes, California, the plantation owners did the same thing here a long time ago. They came when the land was cheap and bought a lot of it. We can do it out west and get more land than they did. Michel writes about beautiful land as far as you can see in a big river valley and–"

"No Will! What about...*civilization*? Why is George Town so bad? Do you have any idea how far California is from here?"

Will raised his voice. "Look Miles, if we stay here, we'll always wonder what could have been if we had only gone west. Someone else is going to get that land if we don't get it first."

There was an awkward silence between the two friends for about a hundred yards. Then they came upon a very large plantation on their left. Miles kept glancing at it as he rode. "So, do we simply join up with others going west?"

"That seems to be what people are trying to do, but I think it's better to travel with people who have the same goal or act like a team. I don't know – that may be too much to ask. We may just have to do it ourselves."

"I knew this day would come."

"You'll live – I promise."

Riding toward town, they began passing some of their neighbor's homes. Several property owners were going back and forth to their houses because it was lunch time. Suddenly from the Hinrich's farm, they saw Elizabeth running toward them with Katherine behind her in tears. Miles and Will turned their horses and ran them to her. Will said, "Elizabeth, what's wrong?"

"Joseph's gone to kill Greeley! He's got a lawsuit against our property!"

Miles pulled the front of his hat down and said, "We'll catch him. Let's go!" Both men kicked their horses into a dead run.

Other neighbors on both sides of the road saw their horses running and knew something was wrong. Some ran to saddle their own horses. Gretchen McConnell was riding at the front of a buckboard wagon with her family on Cross Street going to town. Her son Sammy threw something out of the back of their wagon. She tapped her husband on the shoulder and said, "Clyde, he's doing it again."

Clyde McConnell stiffened his lower lip – looked back at Sammy and raised his voice. "This is your last chance young–"

Gretchen saw Will and Miles shoot down the main road on their horses.

"Clyde – look! I think something's happened with the Hinrich's. They're up there on the road."

Clyde shook his reins and their wagon lurched forward. When they reached Elizabeth and Katherine, he pulled the horses to a stop. Everyone covered their eyes because of the large dust cloud the horses and wagon made. Clyde said, "What happened?"

"It's Joseph!" Elizabeth shouted. "He's going after Greeley!"

Will still couldn't see Joseph. He had to go faster, so he grabbed the saddle horn and whipped Millie on her withers with the reins. As they rode, he yelled to Miles, "He has to be on this road until he hits Main Street! Joseph must've snapped!"

Miles shouted, "I know – I'm leaving you now because Greeley's men will kill him!" Then Chipper showed his real speed and pulled away.

Will yelled, "Go Miles Go! I think I see him!" and thought *come on you slow horse!* Chipper, however, was one of the fastest horses in Scott County, but they were only half a mile from town.

Joseph looked back and saw a familiar tan hat and rider seemingly glued flat over Chipper's back and gaining very fast. He tried kicking his mare, but knew he couldn't outrun Miles.

Miles was beside him after fifty more yards and shouted, "Stop Joseph! You're going to get yourself killed. Elizabeth told us what happened!"

"I don't care. I've had it!"

"They'll kill you first, you fool. Think of your daughter!"

Joseph's mare turned her head briefly to look at Chipper and went off stride, so Miles quickly reached down and grabbed her left rein. Then he leaned back in the saddle with his heels against Chipper's stirrups and pulled hard on both sets of reins. As soon as the horses stopped, Miles grabbed Joseph's shirt collar and yanked him off the saddle. Joseph tried to hold onto his pistol and brace his fall at the same time, but failed.

Will came up from behind them – hopped off Millie from his left stirrup and yelled, "Leave the gun on the ground Joseph or I'll kick your ass!" Then he ran toward Joseph as fast as he could.

Joseph shouted, "Stay out of this Will!" and crawled like an animal to get the pistol, but Will beat him to it and kicked it away. Miles and Will assumed that the fight was over, but Joseph sprang up and swung a fist at Will's face. Will blocked the punch with his forearm and popped Joseph on the nose with his right fist. Joseph fell backwards onto the ground and sat up holding his nose.

Miles pointed far down the road and said, "Oh my god – here they all come."

Will saw a wagon, several men on horses and a large amount of dust following them. "Shit Miles! They can't see Joseph like this. We've got to get him outta here. Give me a hand quick."

They dragged Joseph to a wooded area and tied his hands behind a tree with Miles' belt. Joseph sat in silence with his head down for a few minutes, then Will said, "We all care about you. We know how you feel, but we aren't going to let you get killed by Greeley's men. You've got a family that loves you."

After another minute, Joseph was in tears. He looked up and slowly said, "You're right Will – you're right...I'm sorry."

"Hell Joseph – Greeley probably hoped you'd come gunning for him so he could kill you in self-defense."

Miles saw the throng of neighbors had arrived, so he ran out of the cluster of trees waving his arms yelling, "It's okay! Everything's all right. Joseph is safe. We're talking to him in the trees over there. Give us a moment."

As Miles spoke, more men on horseback rode up and gathered around them. Clyde McConnell spoke first. "We know what happened to Joseph and Elizabeth. Anyone of us could be next. We're not going to stand for it any longer Miles. We're meeting at the courthouse steps tonight."

Miles raised his voice and gestured, "You all go organize whatever you want, but give Joseph and his family some privacy for now."

"Well Miles, something's got to be done!"

"Good go do it – but can you wait a minute? I've got to talk with Elizabeth."

Katherine asked, "Is daddy all right?"

Miles reached into the wagon and gave her a hug. "Yes sweetheart, your daddy's fine. He just hurt his nose that's all." Then he held Elizabeth's hand and helped her down from the wagon. When they were far enough away from the others he said, "I'm not letting everyone know this because I don't want to embarrass Joseph."

"Is he alright?"

Yes, but we had to get physical with him and it wasn't pretty. We've all had times that should be private, and this is one of those times.

"He's hurt isn't he?"

"His nose could be broken." Elizabeth seemed like she would cry, so

Miles gently placed his hand on her shoulder. "I'm sorry Elizabeth. He had that gun and just wouldn't quit.

If anyone asks, let's just say that Joseph fell off his horse and hurt his nose when he hit the ground okay? We'll have him home in a couple of hours."

She gave Miles a hug and said, "Thank you. I know you saved his life."

After Miles knew everyone had left, he went back to Joseph and Will. Joseph was still tied to the tree, but they were both laughing and tears were running down their faces. "What the hell did you tell him Will?"

"Oh nothing...just that it looks like Joseph's going to have even a bigger nose than you!"

Miles looked up and rolled his eyes. "Here we go again – always with the nose. Untie him Will. I talked to Clyde and the others over there."

Joseph said, "The others?"

"Yes, there are a lot of people that care about you Joseph, but they aren't going to know what happened here unless you tell them."

"I know I lost my head Miles, but I hate that man. That's *my* house. It's all we've got."

"Everyone realizes that. You aren't the only one that feels this way. Clyde McConnell has organized a meeting at the courthouse tonight."

The temperature that evening dropped twenty degrees, so most everyone gathered at the courthouse steps wore coats. The people didn't really care about the weather though, because most of them were mad. This meeting also seemed to have added importance because a couple of large plantation owners were present. They rarely came to gatherings the smaller farmers organized unless there was an opportunity that benefited them. Large plantation owners didn't really have to worry about Greeley because they had a safety net against newcomers like him. He was not yet ingratiated into the private lives of the judges in the county court system like the richest landowners and hated this fact.

The children were left to run and play in the street next to the courthouse. Clyde McConnell, a horse enthusiast and prominent miller in the community, winked at Gretchen who was sitting next to him, then walked to the top of the courthouse steps and shouted, "I am glad you all have come." Then he suddenly stopped speaking when a black carriage pulled by four horses stopped in front of the crowd. The driver, whose well-tailored suit belied his low intelligence, climbed down from the carriage, shielded his eyes from the sun, and opened the door for the passengers. Two large men slowly exited the carriage for all to see. One of the men, who appeared to not have a neck because of his large trapezii, was dressed in a gray suit and stepped down to the street first. The next man that exited wore a very dark suit with pin stripes. This one also appeared very strong, but had a scar on his face. He looked over the crowd and focused on the speaker at the top of the stairs. Clyde McConnell looked across the crowd at the scar-faced man with an intent stare. The crowd became silent. Then voices muttered *Greeley...*

From another side of the crowd, Will, Miles, Joseph, Elizabeth and little Katherine walked to the steps of the courthouse. Joseph had a bandage on his nose. Will looked up at Clyde and shouted for all to hear, "Please Clyde continue!" Clyde looked up and began to speak. Will and Miles, however, didn't look at Clyde. They turned their backs to him and looked out at the crowd in Greeley's direction.

Clyde shouted again. "Our way of life and work is being endangered by an evil man consumed with greed. This man has tried to take advantage of honest purchasers of land like myself and Joseph here. He's trying to kick out families that have farmed this area for years." Then Clyde pointed to the scar-faced man in the pinstriped suit. "This man is here tonight. He is none other than Anton Greeley! Well Mr. Greeley, we're not going to stand for it anymore. I say we band together to defeat this thief who has come to our good community to steal our land!" Joseph stood up and raised his hands above his head to clap. A cheer went out for him because most people heard what happened earlier in the day.

Greeley couldn't stand it. He left his body guard and rushed through the crowd pushing others aside. Some of the citizens gathered were peaceful farmers and had not seen behavior like this firsthand. Another group of men saw what was happening and tried to get through the crowd to stop Greeley.

Right before Greely started up the stairs, Miles grabbed him by the shoulder, spun him around, and said, "You haven't been invited to speak!" Greeley hit Miles with a very quick left fist to the stomach then a right fist to the nose. Miles fell backwards onto Katherine, who screamed.

Then Greeley started up the stairs toward Clyde. Will took two long strides and jumped all the way to the porch. Greeley said, "Out of my way shit kicker!" and swung his right fist at Will's face. Will raised his left arm and blocked Greeley's punch. Greeley's eyes widened, and before he had another thought, Will's right fist hit him in the middle of the nose breaking it. Greeley flew backwards from the top of the stairs to the ground. The people behind him scrambled to get out of the way. His rear end hit the ground first, followed by the back of his head. The body guard finally reached Greeley and tried to revive him, but couldn't and waived for the driver.

Then everyone fell silent.

Will took the opportunity to speak in a loud unwavering voice. "My name is Will Richards. Besides what Clyde just said, I want something different than fighting this dressed up cheat! Live for yourselves. Don't live to battle people like this. There will always be a time to fight and a time to walk away." He gestured with his right arm down at the unconscious Anton Greeley. "He is not worth your time!"

Clyde McConnell thought of the fear on Elizabeth's face from earlier in the day and yelled out, "He's right! Greeley's not worth it!"

Then the crowd shouted, "Wake up Greeley! Wake up Greeley!"

Will motioned with his hands to get the crowd's attention and yelled, "I don't like him either. Mock him all you want. Pool your money and beat him once or twice in court. What will happen then? Greeley will either quit and move on or try harder. Let's say Greeley loses and moves on."

"That'll be great!" shouted another one of the mill owners.

Will recognized the miller's input by turning to him and pointing. Then he quickly looked up and shouted, "Okay – then what happens next? The land titles will still be a problem! There's a lot of *Greeley's* in this world. Another richer Greeley will come along and try the same thing again." Will's raised his voice. "Either way, you will have spent another year or two in this area and your crops will yield less and less. Aren't we already having that problem now?"

Everyone suddenly became quiet.

Clyde leaned over to Will and whispered, "What in the world are you talking about?"

Will quietly said, "You'll see," then shouted while waving his arm in Greeley's direction. "There's a bigger picture than the unconscious man lying before you. The soil here is already getting used up. More people from the East are arriving here every day to compete with you. Between the new farmers and the plantation owners, you'll eventually be squeezed, and the crops you have will be worthless."

Creighton MacTavish, adorned with an elaborate hat, was one of the well-dressed plantation owners in attendance. He raised a hand to his friend, who had been making a crude comment about another farmer in the crowd, and quietly said in a dignified tone, "Lawrence – hush yawl mouth this instant – there may be more land coming up for sale out of all this."

Will went on. "Listen – the problem is the big property owners got to this area first and that's not going to change, but we can do the same! We need to go to a place where we are first and *we* are the ones settling large acreages of land like the plantation owners did. That place is far west of here and we have that opportunity right now!" Will lowered his voice. "Everyone here is going to live and die on this earth. At least, live for something greater than this. Instead of pooling money for a fight here that is going nowhere, let's pool our money for a better existence for us all. I have a place for us to go where we will live under the shadow of no one!"

Whatever had happened to the crowd, be it Greeley getting knocked out, or the words they heard after that, the people quietly looked at Will. Many had never considered such a drastic move. When Will stopped talking, the crowd cheered, "To hell with Greeley! To hell with Greeley!"

Because of the all the noise, the Town Marshall and

members of the Night Watch arrived on horses. Greeley's driver and the no-neck bodyguard were at his side. No one else had moved to help him since he hit the ground. Greeley suddenly awoke and touched his face with his right hand. He could tell that his nose had been bleeding. He also saw Will Richards standing above him at the top of the courthouse steps, and without thinking twice, reached for a pistol under his coat. Then, the sound of a gunshot echoed throughout the courthouse area. Greeley looked toward the direction of the shot, and saw the Marshall quickly holstering one pistol and pointing another directly at him.

Greeley's bodyguard whispered in his ear, "Easy Anton, we don't have the law in this town yet – remember?"

Greeley whispered slowly to the men at his side "What's the name of the person that hit me? I will kill him."

His bodyguard whispered, "Will Richards."

The Marshall shouted, "You there, on the ground with the gun! Put it on the ground – stand up and move back from it!" Greeley slowly complied. The Marshall shouted again. "You men – leave now. You may come to my office later next week to discuss how you might be able to regain your firearm."

Greeley walked slowly behind his men while holding a bloody handkerchief to his nose. The bodyguard held open the carriage door for his boss. Greeley motioned to the driver and bodyguard to both get to the top of the carriage. Greeley slowly climbed into the passenger compartment without assistance. His driver released the brake, grabbed the reins and slapped them on the horse's backs. The carriage slowly started down the street.

Clyde smirked and walked to Will saying, "That beautiful horse-drawn carriage exit looked like a dog limping away with its tail between its legs, but this isn't the end of it. You better watch your back."

Will put his arm around Clyde's shoulder. "I'm not afraid of him." Then Will turned and shouted at the crowd, "For those of you interested in what I said tonight – come to my house at four o'clock next Saturday." With that, he stepped down from the courthouse stairs, gave Katherine and Elizabeth a hug, shook Joseph's hand and quietly said, "It all changes now, Joseph. I want you and your family to come with us. I will help you. You won't be sorry."

Joseph smiled from under his nose bandage. The crowd began talking among themselves.

Will said, "Come on Miles, let's go."

On their way back home, Miles said, "Damn Will. It looks like you're getting the team you wanted."

"Maybe. We first have to see the number of people that are truly interested. It's one thing for them to get worked up after a speech. It's quite another for people to leave everything they have and risk their lives walking all the way across North America."

The short carriage ride back to Greeley's mansion was very quiet. Greeley sat alone in the carriage's back seat and gripped the door handle tighter and tighter until his left hand went numb. With his right hand, he held a bloodied white handkerchief to his nose. He knew he would have two black eyes from Will Richard's blow because his nose was broken. He had been through this before when he was a young fighter. He kept thinking over and over *I have never been beaten like that.*

When the carriage stopped, he felt a knot on the back of his head and grimaced. He would still have to climb two flights of stairs before he could be alone. Going up the stairs, his also felt a sharp pain in his left heel and realized that he must have somehow injured it in the fall as well.

His carriage driver and bodyguard waited downstairs but did not say a word. They knew better than to approach Anton Greeley or even speak to him during times like this. After Greeley ascended the stairs, he walked almost calmly. Adorning an antique table in the middle of his entry hall was a beautiful crystal vase that had been in his family for decades. Greeley clutched the vase in his right hand and threw it as hard as he could down the lengthy hallway. It impacted on the heavy trim above the doorway to the grand living room and shattered into smithereens. His driver and bodyguard downstairs heard the crash and ran up the stairs to see what was wrong.

Greeley continued walking. The bottom of his shoes crushed the broken crystal on the floor beneath his feet. Upon reaching the threshold of the ornate living room, he saw Spivey urinating in front of a heavy wooden chair and directly onto the large Oriental rug that covered the entire room. The dog was apparently startled by the noise or was demonstrating his true feelings toward his master. Greeley's eyes bulged from their sockets. He ran at the dog, pulled his right leg back, and in one long stride, swung his right foot forward to kick poor Spivey. The agile terrier easily dodged Greeley's foot which landed hard into the bottom of the heavy chair. Greeley went down in a heap onto the rug holding his right foot while screaming and rolling on the damp urine stain.

The bodyguard was first into the room and quickly asked what happened? Are you all right?

Greeley laid on the ground with his right arm over his eyes. After a few seconds, he muttered. "I'm going to kill him. I'm going to kill him!"

"Spivey?" asked the dimwitted driver.

Greeley pulled his arm back from his swollen blood-shot eyes and shouted "No! You Idiot!... Richards! I'm going to have Richards killed if it's the last thing I ever do."

CHAPTER TWO
ADDING TO THE
CAUSE

The crowd at the courthouse slowly dispersed. Some groups of people still lingered to visit about the prospect of going west. Their discussions dealt with articles people had read about the West that painted two very different pictures. One was a story of desolation and a journey filled with danger. The other described bountiful farm lands, big blue skies, and picturesque mountains that could be seen from fifty miles away.

On their way back home on Cross Street, Will said, "You okay? Greeley snuck one in on you back there."

Miles placed his right fist against his right nostril and blew his left nostril hard sending blood and mucus onto the ground. Then he repeated the effort for his right nostril. "I'm better off than Greeley. You put him down pretty good, Will." Then Miles hocked and spit. "How many do you think will come?"

"I don't know, but I meant what I said."

Miles spit again. "Who else has the money to do this?"

"You don't sound good, Miles. You think Greeley broke that beak of yours?"

"Shut up Will, I'm fine. Who else do we know with money is coming?"

"We're starting a community, Miles. What we need to do is start picking who we want to contribute, but we've also got to make it there without getting killed."

"Sounds like we're footing some bills. What do we *really* know about walking all the way to California? Why don't we just take a ship to where we need to go?"

"I thought about that, but Michel also said in his letter to *not* take a ship around South America and don't try cutting across Central America."

"Why not? Wouldn't it be better than walking the whole way?"

"The people that got off those ships said the conditions were horrible. Some tried cutting through Central America. They were eaten alive by mosquitos crossing a jungle and had to wait weeks for a ship to pick them up when they got to the Pacific."

"No! What if we start sailing from the Eastern Seaboard and stayed *on* the ship?"

Miles was getting ahead because Chipper walked faster than Millie. Will kicked Millie a little to catch up. "Miles, he said that the people that traveled on ships were trapped in wretched conditions for six months no matter which way they went. It didn't sound good."

Miles began to slow and simply stared at the ground as Chipper walked.

Will pulled slightly on Millie's reins so Chipper could catch up. "It's not a cake walk, Miles. He wrote that the best way to do it is to get to Fort John, and he will help us from there. It's not going to be that bad."

"What about the Indians out there? What about our own baths and beds? What about life as we know it?"

"You're a baby. Stop whining. We've all camped before. We ride steamboats on the rivers to West Port anyway."

"I can't believe it. You've been way too quiet recently. I knew something was happening."

"You can stay here and live your safe little mediocre

life if you want, but I'm going."

"My destiny is to die young. I finally understand that now."

"Shut up, Miles. Right now we just need the right people."

"Who – Ian?"

"He's the best shot in the county. He can't hurt."

"Yes he can. You never know what kind of mood he's going to be in. He could be a giant pain in the ass."

"He is single and doesn't really have any large ties to George Town. We can make it worth his while maybe?"

"No, I believe he'll shoot down anything that looks like we need him. He has to want to do this himself. Let's just talk to him. Tell him what we're doing – and see what happens."

"We still need more than Ian though."

"I know – the other person that could really help us is Nate."

"Your buddy Nate already has a great business here. Why would he go?"

"I don't know – his family has to really want to go or they won't do it. We need him. He can build the town where we're going and can help us get there because he's good with a gun and everything else he plays with out at his house."

"Remember, though, he is a freedman with many ties here. People look up to him because of where he's come from. Do you see that beautiful wife of his and their child traipsing across North America?"

"So what! Everyone's come from somewhere. We're going, and he's my friend, so I'm asking him. If he says no – he says no."

Miles quietly sighed. "Okay, you go talk to Nate first. I'll go to Ian's shop, but you have to get there as soon as you can."

"So you're facing Ian's lecture tomorrow first – and not me – right?"

"There'll be plenty of Ian left for you."

"Miles – decline the whisky okay? Things will go easier."

"What if they both don't want to go?"

"We'll still pick up help on the trail."

"Michel's bunch?"

"Yeah, in the end Michel and his bunch are going to get us through this."

The next day, Will rode Millie to Nathaniel Hamilton's place of business in the southwest part of George Town. Nathaniel, or "Nate" as all his friends called him, was of African descent and widely regarded as the best builder in all of George Town. As Will rode, he attempted to come to terms with the fact that if Nate did not want to travel west, they would probably never see each other again. Nathaniel and his family lived in a two-story house. Behind it was a large open area for building supplies, wagons and a barn. When Will came upon the property, he saw Nate holding a hatchet in his hand. When he threw it, the hatchet rotated end over end and stuck into a massive tree stump that had been propped on its side for a target. He repeated this several times with a pile of hatchets lying by his feet. Then he reached for a set of knives next to them. Will saw that he was working up a sweat and shouted, "Nate – you're a busy man today I see...should I come back later?" A brown wrinkle-faced bloodhound named Samson began howling and ran to Will and Millie.

Nate looked over his shoulder and squinted because the sun was behind Will's head. "Looks like that sun is lighting up some of that white hair from under your hat.

It's a little early for you, isn't it?"

Will slowly dismounted Millie. Then knelt and petted Samson for an unusual amount of time before answering. "At least I've still got some hair."

Nate frowned. "That was kind of weak, big man – even coming from you. What's wrong?"

Will looked up. "Oh nothing – let's go blasting. We need to talk."

"But Abigail already has lunch."

"C'mon Nate, you Abagail and Caleb still need dinner don't you?"

Nate looked toward his house. "Okay, but she's not going to be happy. Give me a minute. My rifle's in the bedroom."

"Just tell her you're going hunting."

"She's not in a good mood right now. That's *kind of* why I'm out here."

"I'll pray for you, my friend."

"Doing what I can – you owe me, big man." Nate walked quickly and quietly to the back door. Once he was in the house, he glanced toward the kitchen and saw Abigail and their four-year-old boy, Caleb, standing on a stool and helping his mother prepare lunch. Believing that his wife and young son were otherwise involved, he tiptoed toward the bedroom.

Abigail Hamilton thought she heard something and poked her head out of the kitchen. She looked first to the back door then to the bedroom and saw Nate walking on his toes with his back to her. She quickly came out of the kitchen, got behind Nate, and said loudly, "He's here again isn't he?"

An odd loud sound came out of Nate's mouth as he shook and fell forward toward a chair in the middle of the room, but he raised his arms and caught himself before falling. "Jesus Abby! You almost gave me a heart attack."

"Heart attack – my butt! I see you sneaking around – skipping out on lunch again."

"You sneaking around again, Daddy?" was little Caleb's question, as he peered around door frame of the kitchen.

Nate was breathing heavily, so he sat in the chair, looked up at his wife and said, "We still need food for dinner though, Abby – right?"

"Don't you Abby me! You hunting with him only means *I'll* be cleaning a bunch of dead squirrels!"

Nate took a couple of deep breaths. "I know Will. Something's different with him today. He didn't come here to hunt. It's an excuse, I think, to talk about something else – something serious."

Abigail's tone changed. "I hope he's okay. I'll come out and say hello while you get over your heart attack."

Nate slowly stood. "All right, I'll get my rifle. See what the man has to say if you can."

Will was holding a hatchet when Abigail came outside. He tried throwing it at the tree stump, but it rotated wildly and missed the stump entirely.

"It does take some practice."

"Oh...hi Abigail. You look great today. Nate's a very lucky man isn't he?"

"Yes he is. Now cut the bull and tell me what's going on."

"You cut to the chase don't you?"

"Yes I do."

"I have some things I'm considering in my life right now and wanted to see what Nate thought."

"You aren't sick are you?"

"No I'm fine. It's a business decision."

"Like what?"

"Going west."

Abigail stared at Will for a few moments. "You're out of your mind, aren't you?"

"Nope."

Nate came out of the house with his rifle. Abigail walked toward him and said loud enough for Will to hear, "You were right. It's something serious. Talk some sense into him."

Nate saddled his horse, Dominick, and whistled for Samson before they walked to a nearby wooded area. Nate was still quiet until they approached the trees. "All right, big man, you told Abigail. Now you tell me."

"Remember a while back when we were hunting and I talked about the idea of going west, and you told me something like *it sounds great but was it worth it?*"

A politely concerned smile came over Nate's face. "Uh...kind of. Your mouth ran a lot that day. Why?"

"It's no longer talk, Nate. I've heard from a good friend of mine who's a trapper. He just bought more than 8000 river valley acres in California."

"How much did he pay?"

"A fraction of what Miles and my places cost combined."

Dominick took a few more steps before Nate said, "Well, looky here!" Will turned his head and saw two squirrels leaping from one branch to the next. Nate, however, wasn't prepared to shoot, so he quickly hopped off Dominick and went through the process of charging and capping his rifle, but before he could do anything else, the squirrels ran away. "Damn Will! That's the first thing that *always* happens when we get here!"

"You actually cursed Nate. I'm offended – but when've you ever shot one of the little beggars from a damned horse?"

"What? I am capable of shooting a squirrel from the back of a horse, but I will be entering the gates of hell *far* behind you and your mouth."

"Not as long as I've been hunting with you, you haven't. C'mon, let's tie the horses to those trees and do this right."

After tying their horses to trees, they walked quietly into the forest with their rifles. Then Nate whispered, "So, your friend got himself a lot of land out west?"

"Nate, Miles and I would be crazy not to do the same thing."

"You're going then?"

"We're going, and we want you and your family to come with us."

Nate snapped the fingers on his free hand. "Yeah just like that – take my family – leave my business and walk across the continent because you got a letter from an old friend?"

"I know Nate. It's a lot to ask, but Miles and I are doing it, and we have others coming too. You're one of my best friends, so how was I not going to ask you?"

"California, Will? Come on."

"I know – It almost seems crazy, but I see the opportunity."

"You can die trying."

Will remained quiet for several moments, then somberly said, "Nate, I want you to come, but you have a life here and people respect what you do. I understand either way."

Nate stopped walking, and looked at the ground, then he turned toward Will with tears in his eyes. "Will, it might look like our family is doing well, but life here, for me, has not been that pleasant. I want to have a relationship with everyone here like I have with you."

"I understand."

"No... you don't. Many of my friends are still slaves, so I'm getting very tired of catering to certain people in this town if you know what I mean. What's happening here isn't right."

"Nate, one day all these states will be different and there will be no slaves. I know it's wrong, but we both have a better opportunity for our lives *right now*. You and your family can help build that community in more ways than one."

Nate rubbed his eyes with his shirtsleeve. "I don't know if going west is the answer, Will."

"Only you and your family can answer that. Talk to them. Think about their future over the next ten years living here or living out there. We're all meeting at my place next Saturday afternoon."

Nate's rifle was pointed at the ground for a few moments, as he listened to Will, then he asked, "All?"

"Anyone that wants to come. We'll probably join a wagon train in West Port."

Nate extended his hand. "You know Will – I really don't feel like hunting anymore."

Will shook his hand. "I really never did. It was always about this."

"I'll talk to Abby."

"This is a big deal, Nate, I know, but for our lives right now, I think it's best that we do this. Let me know."

"I will."

Nate hopped on Dominick and Samson followed them back to their house. Will wondered how Miles was doing with Ian MacGregor and made his way to Ian's shop on the west side of town. When he entered the small living area of the shop, he saw Miles sitting on one of two small chairs next to an old wooden rectangular table with a pile of clothes on it. Will sat down and whispered, "Where's Ian? Has he been drinking?"

"A little – I think. He went to the other room to get a tool."

Will looked at what appeared to be a ladies' garment in the pile of clothes. "Do you think the old man is seeing someone?"

"Don't ask him *that* whatever you do. That's his kilt – the Clan MacGregor. I've already gotten a lecture on it."

"No wonder he always wears that long dark coat if that's what's on underneath. That's got to be cold."

"How did it go with Nate?"

Will shrugged and looked to see if Ian was coming, "We'll see. He's going to talk to Abigail."

Miles leaned over to Will and whispered, "If *Nate* actually trusts your California pipe dream, maybe your idea isn't so bad after all."

"Like I said before – you can stay here if you like."

Ian suddenly walked in, and in a loud heavy Scottish accent bellowed, "That will be fine, Will. He can stay here with me in George Town because I'm *certainly* not going."

Will looked back at Miles and rolled his eyes.

"That's obviously what you both have come here for, right? It certainly wasn't for your rifle, Miles. There is nothing wrong with that gun! Wish I could say the same for your nose and black eyes."

"Never mind Miles. He had a little dust up – how do you know you don't want to go, Ian? Let's have a bourbon together, and I'll tell you the plan!"

"Ha – the only thing I have here is simple *whisky* unless we can prove that it actually came from our neighbors in *Bourbon County.*"

"Bourbon is bourbon. I don't care what our neighbors have to say. Let me tell you where we're going."

"What do I need to know other than you're going to be walking across North America – living on biscuits and bacon with only a small glimmer of hope of reaching your destination alive!"

"I don't care. We need you Ian."

Ian saw Miles' jaw drop. Then Ian stroked his beard and raised his voice again. "You need another person that can handle a rifle. That's really the only reason you're here isn't it?"

"Yes."

"Well Will, I knew that was the case when–"

Will interrupted. "I thought you would have loved the adventure, but I was obviously wrong Ian. I came to tell you about a meeting we are having, but if you want to spend the rest of your life here, that's fine. We, however, are going to see the west – sorry to have bothered you." Will stood, motioned to Miles, and walked out Ian's front door. Miles followed him out and gently shut the door behind them.

When they got to their horses, they saw Ian with only his head protruding from the front door shouting, "And another thing, I heard about your meeting! Better pack a lot of dough so your damned biscuits don't run out!"

Will quietly said, "Don't look back Miles, keep moving."

Ian continued to scream from the doorway. "You'll never make it through Indian Territory alive! I don't need a meeting to tell me that!"

Miles and Will kept their backs to Ian and kept walking to their horses. "He's just getting started, Will."

"I know. Ignore him. Get on your horse." After Will and Miles started to ride away, Ian only yelled louder, "If the Indians don't get you, you'll all die of thirst in the desert!"

Ian's voice eventually faded away the further they rode and Will said, "I guess we can count Ian in too."

"After that?" said Miles.

"Yes after that! We don't leave till spring. He wants us to bow to him and scrape the ground with our back foot a few times, but he's coming. I promise. He already knew what life would be like on the trail, and he knew about the meeting. He just wanted to argue, Miles."

"This is going to be an interesting winter, Will."

"We're going to have people coming with us that we actually know *and like*. You know what else? We're going need a few more good horses for this. It's not going to hurt the cause either if we pick up one for Ian too."

"So we go from his tirade to getting him a new horse? Even for Ian, that's a little more than just bowing and scraping."

"Do you have a better idea right now? Besides, I know just where to find them. You remember the Hendrickson's farm, right?"

CHAPTER THREE
THE STALLION

The Hendrickson's horse farm on North Elk Horn Creek was located west of George Town. Will had been all over the northern part of Kentucky looking at horses during his life in George Town and the Hendrickson's always had the best selection. Will and Miles left their houses at dawn and met on West Main Street. Miles saw Will riding toward him and yelled, "You're still looking for a horse better than Chipper aren't you?"

"You sound like a second grader Miles – grow up."

Miles smiled because Will knew he was right, so he shouted back. "Why is this horse trip going to be any different from Louisville or that huge waste of time in Cincinnati?"

"I'm not looking for a race horse! We just need decent horses for this trip Miles – that's all. The Hendrickson's will have what we want."

"When was the last time you even saw Jacobus?"

"It's been a long time – you know how busy I've been."

Miles slowly walked Chipper up to Will and Millie. "I don't think I've seen them since they lost that horse."

"I heard about that. It sounded horrible. Anyway – hope you brought a change of clothes because this could take a day or two depending on what we see."

After a long ride, they came upon tall trees lining both sides of Elk Horn Creek and felt cooler breezes now that autumn had arrived. Every time Will saw this part of the creek, he thought about the times when he and his father canoed here when he was a child.

"Will, what in the world are you thinking about?"

"Oh...my dad and the things he used to say when we were on this creek."

"Like what?"

Will pointed to an area of the creek and said, "One day the creek was running fast and the current down there jammed our canoe up against that little island in the middle. I was afraid and my dad told me, "If you ever get into trouble out here, William, stay calm. Most of the time your feet can still touch the bottom." Then Will rubbed tears from his eyes with his shirtsleeve.

"It's okay Will. I think about my dad too. It's life. None of us lives forever."

Will cleared his throat a couple of times and said, "I know Miles."

After that, they rode in silence for a long time before the road to the Hendrickson's farm finally came into view. Will saw several horses running in a pasture by the creek. There were quarter horses and a black horse that appeared to be a thoroughbred mix. What really caught Will's eye, though, was the power this horse possessed. As they came closer, Will could see this fast horse was a stallion. He watched him chase other horses weaving through the trees and couldn't believe how nimble he was in tight spaces. Then, when he ran into an open field, his strides lengthened and allowed him to cover a lot of ground when he ran at top speed.

"Miles, that Stallion has can run down every other horse in the pasture from behind, either through those trees or out in the open."

"It's like he always has to prove that he's the fastest,

Will."

"My guess is he's at least sixteen hands high and older than a yearling."

"Look how the sun reflects off the black coat when he runs too."

"I know. I love that splash of white on his nose."

The road into the farm was tree lined with fenced pastures on either side and stretched for half a mile up to the main house.

Miles said, "Hey there's Sarah!"

Sarah Hendrickson was a woman in her fifties with greying dark hair and striking features. She was on the front porch and saw riders approaching but couldn't tell who they were. When Will got closer, he yelled, "Sarah it's me – Will Richards!"

She yelled back, "Will Richards, I almost didn't recognize you. Where have you been for the past couple of years?"

Will thought, *had it really been that long*? He rode closer to the porch and hopped off Millie. "Sarah, I haven't been a very good friend. I should have come by sooner."

She didn't respond, but instead quickly said, "Hello Miles, I guess you men are looking for Jacobus?"

Miles said, "Yes, we're looking for horses today. How is Jacobus?"

"It's not been good, Miles. He's never been the same since we lost Hawkeye. He's been blaming himself."

"That's not like Jacobus he–"

Sarah interrupted. "He's not the same person you knew."

"Sarah, I'm sorry. I heard that you lost that beautiful horse a while back." Sarah looked down and didn't answer. Will could see she was upset. "It's okay Sarah, I'll find Jacobus."

"He's down at the stables."

Will decided to let Miles talk to her alone. "Thank you Sarah. I'll talk to him. Maybe we can help." When Will walked away, he glanced at Miles intently before leaving them to find Jacobus. Miles knew this look meant that he needed to keep talking to Sarah.

As Will approached the stables, he wanted to see his old friend just as he remembered and yelled, "Jacobus! It's me Will! Are you in there?" Jacobus heard his voice and walked toward him. They shook hands, but Jacobus's eyes quickly darted away.

Will could see what Sarah was talking about. The Jacobus that Will remembered was a stout man with piercing eyes and blond hair. Will noticed that he had aged much more than he should have in two years and thought, *I can't bring back a dead horse.* Will decided to ignore what Sarah said and simply talk to Jacobus as he had in the past. "I saw a black stallion out there and was wondering if he was for sale?"

"Ha! Many have tried to ride that horse this past year and none have succeeded."

"Maybe they weren't that good, Jacobus."

"No, I've come to believe that some horses are not meant to be ridden Will – and if that's the case, they should simply live out their lives in a state of nature as the Lord intended."

Will immediately thought, *Jacobus has had way too much time on his hands.* "Perhaps some horses only like being with certain people Jacobus. We just don't know if a horse and a person are meant to be with each other until it happens."

"This stallion has broken two collarbones and a femur on three people that thought the same way you do.

What's going to make you different? Is it going to be worth a broken collarbone and no horse?"

"Jacobus, is he for sale or not?"

"No!"

"What's happened to you, Jacobus?"

Jacobus turned his back to Will and shoveled muck out of a stall for a couple of minutes. Will watched him and thought, *is he going to cry?* Then Jacobus rested the shovel against a stall and said, "I can't stop thinking about Hawkeye. It doesn't seem as bad when I see Lucky out there in the pasture, so I think he will live out his days here."

"What? I love horses like you do, Jacobus, but you've got to get past this or you're going to lose Sarah too."

"We're fine Will. It's just tough right now."

"Well, you don't look fine and neither does Sarah. When was the last time you bought or sold a horse?" Jacobus did not answer. Will waited for Jacobus to look at him again. "I want to help you, Jacobus. I'll pay twice what you think that stallion is worth just for the *chance* to ride him!"

"You can't be serious."

"Oh, I'm serious all right. You need to make a deal. You can't lose! If I do ride him, he's mine, but no matter what happens – you get double the money."

"You're crazy, Will. He's worth a lot."

"I don't care. If it's meant to be, it's meant to be. If not, I'll have to live with that fact, but I'm willing to try. How about you Jacobus – what are you afraid of?"

"Let me think about it, Will."

"You're the one putting *yourself* out to pasture and not that damned stallion, Jacobus."

Jacobus snapped back, "Okay, it's your neck, not mine. Let's go get him. His name is Lucky!"

Will was pleased that he saw a glimpse of the old Jacobus. "Lucky?"

"We named him Lucky because he and Red almost died at birth. We ended up selling the sire before that."

"Boaz?"

"You remember. We needed the money and thought Hawkeye would be with us a lot longer than he was."

"Both were fantastic horses in their prime, Jacobus. I remember them racing at the Commons track."

"Yes they were great – now let's go. I'm getting the halter, lunge line, and a bucket of oats."

"Lunge line – what the hell is that?"

"A young man from France came through here and stayed with us for a few weeks. He said they used to run stubborn horses in a circle before they tried to break them."

"Like a long leash?"

Jacobus picked up what looked like a dark fishing pole with a braided leather handle and a fine whipcord on the end. "Yes, but he had this long whip in the other hand or simply twirled the other end of the line."

"I guess that kept the horses running from *something*?"

"That was the trick – keep them running and get them tired."

"Does it work?"

"Yes, but it takes more time than holding onto the saddle horn and wishing for best while you get bucked."

"Is all that stuff really necessary?"

"Not with most of the horses, but it might be something to try with this one."

"Hell, I'll try it. We need those ropes hanging on those pegs too right?"

"Yep, the ropes and some of those carrots over there

in that bucket."

After walking four hundred yards toward the pen, Jacobus called Lucky's name while he shook a bucket of oats. All the horses in the pasture, however, heard and saw Jacobus shaking the bucket of oats. Lucky continued to buck and kick his hind legs at the other horses, but finally started to walk back to the pen because he also knew there were oats in the bucket. After all the horses were in the pen, Will shut the gate behind them. Jacobus poured oats into several metal bowls on the ground and Will saw an interesting dynamic take place. When the horses started eating the oats, a very young dark quarter horse could not eat because the other horses kept pushing him off any bowl he approached, like a game of musical chairs.

Will leaned over to Jacobus and cutely remarked, "I see there's a pecking order with them."

"Will, this always happens when I try to get only one of them in the pen with oats. You know as well as I do – they all want to come, and as soon as they get in the pen, they begin to act like a pack of dogs. Usually they eat in their barn stalls! If I had known you were coming, I would have had the horse we were working already separated in a barn stall."

Miles walked up on them and shouted from thirty yards away, "Hey can I help?"

Jacobus turned, "How long have you been here Miles? What happened to your face? Did you run into a door?"

"It's really nothing Jacobus...I was talking to Sarah. How have you–"

"Never mind that. We're working a horse." Jacobus handed Miles one of the ropes and said, "Stay outside the pen with this until we need you."

Will asked, "How can I help?"

"You go work the gate, and I will push them to you. Watch Lucky though! He'll try to get to the side of any horse that is running out ahead of him. If he gets out, we'll never get him back. He loves running through the trees from his time with Hawkeye."

Will unlatched the gate and stood behind it. Jacobus grabbed the lunge whip and positioned himself between the pack of horses and the gate, then he skillfully used the lunge whip to separate one horse at a time. Will's job was to open and shut the gate quickly so that Lucky would be the only horse left in the pen. When only Lucky and a bay quarter horse were left, Jacobus approached Lucky with the whip. Lucky reared and started to bring his front feet down toward Jacobus. This was a move Jacobus had seen before, so he stepped back as Lucky reared. After that, in an effort to block Lucky, he held the lunge whip and his free hand toward his nose and yelled, "Now Will, let out the bay!" Will opened the gate. Lucky saw the bay escaping the pen to be with the other horses, so he brought his hooves down and bolted. Jacobus dove to the right and hit the ground. Lucky saw he had only a few more strides to catch the bay.

Jacobus quickly sat up and yelled, "Close the gate Will! Close the gate!"

Will saw Lucky coming fast and pushed the gate shut as quickly as he could, but he was too late. The bay and Lucky wound up almost side by side between the end of the gate and the latch post. The bay was still able to squeeze out of the pen because most of his body was already past the gate. Will used all his strength to push the gate shut and get Lucky back into the pen, but he kept wedging his head through.

Miles saw what was happening and ran right at Lucky from outside the pen. When he was almost at the gate, he took off his hat – jumped in the air and yelled – then swung his hat at Lucky's nose. Lucky was startled by Miles' antics and pulled his head back. Jacobus gradually stood up holding his right elbow and Will pushed hard until the gate latched.

Lucky was trapped, so he galloped twice around the pen and turned directly at Jacobus, again. Jacobus ran to the fence – placed his right foot on the lowest rail – grabbed the top rail and tried to pull himself out, but he was only able to swing his left leg over the top. Lucky caught Jacobus' right leg above his ankle and scraped it mercilessly against the fence. Jacobus cried out in pain and flopped onto the ground outside the pen. Will and Miles ran around the pen to help him. Jacobus was lying on his back holding his right ankle while Lucky continued to run and buck in the pen. Dust was everywhere.

With his eyes shut, Jacobus quietly muttered, "Will, you still want to pay twice the amount for more of that?"

Miles saw a look of shock on Will's face and said, "Will, we've worked a lot of cattle and horses, but I've never seen an animal this fast and this wild."

Will was still breathing hard and sat down. He thought for a second and offered a different tactic. "Why don't we try this in small steps?"

Jacobus opened his eyes and gradually sat up.

Miles shook his head. "Baby steps to what Will – a broken neck? Didn't you see that horse go after Jacobus? Look at him now!" Lucky was just starting to have fun. He continued running and bucking, as if he were celebrating.

Will patted Jacobus on the shoulder and asked, "Do you think we can get a halter and that lunge line on him?"

Jacobus coughed because of all the dust. "Maybe if we can get close enough."

"Let's give it a try – your leg all right?"

Jacobus slowly stood up, holding his right elbow, and hobbled to the lean on a fence rail. "Don't worry about me, Will Richards. I will be fine." Will walked to his jacket, pulled out a carrot, and hopped over the fence into the pen. Lucky was making another lap in the pen, but stopped when he saw the carrot. Jacobus handed the halter and lunge line over the fence to Will, who walked toward the stallion. Lucky stood by the side of the fence opposite from Jacobus and neighed loudly. Will calmly flattened his hand completely so Lucky wouldn't bite his fingers. After Lucky crunched the carrot with his front teeth, Will scratched his forehead and discretely slipped the lunge line over Lucky's neck. Now he was able to hold it in place with one hand like an untied leash. Will was still not convinced that Lucky was going cooperate, so he reached his left hand behind him and gestured for another carrot. Miles saw Will's silent begging and brought another carrot to him. Lucky consumed it as quickly as he did the first and Will thought, *so far so good.* Then, he gently raised the halter to Lucky's head in one hand while he held the lunge line around Lucky's neck with the other. Lucky didn't like the looks of the halter and jerked back. Will tried to hold on, but Lucky pulled him off his feet, Jacobus jumped into the pen as fast as he could and threw another rope around Lucky's neck. Miles ran to get his rope. Lucky jerked hard to one side and started to rear on his hind legs.

Jacobus shouted, "Miles – any time now! He's pulling us off our feet!"

Miles ran back with his rope and threw it over Lucky's neck. Now three ropes were around Lucky's neck but it didn't matter. He continued to drag Will, Miles and Jacobus with him. They did everything they could to hold Lucky for a few more seconds while Will got the halter over Lucky's head. He quickly buckled it and said, "All right give me the whip and let him go." Jacobus and Miles loosened their ropes from Lucky's neck and got out of the pen.

Will coiled some of the lunge line in his left hand and moved to the center of the pen. Lucky ran forward, but the rope was attached to a metal ring on the halter just under his mouth. He could run, but only as far as the lunge line allowed. He became frustrated and wanted to run faster, but Will stayed in one place keeping Lucky running from right to left. He held the whip in his right hand, but never had to use it because Lucky was content to keep running. After ten minutes of running right to left, Lucky began sweating and breathing hard with an occasional snort and shake of his head. This was all new to Lucky. He could run all he wanted but it wasn't the same as before. He was directed now. After twenty minutes passed, Will ran Lucky for another twenty minutes in the opposite direction. Even for a horse with Lucky's stamina, the constant pace finally wore him down.

Miles asked Jacobus, "What do you think?"

"It looks like they have an understanding now, Miles. Will's no longer a stranger." Then Jacobus shouted, "That ought to do it for today Will."

"I hear you Jacobus – that's it for him."

"Okay Will...would you like to walk him to his stall in the barn *now* or turn him out in the pasture and repeat all this tomorrow as well?"

"All right! I'll never come here unannounced again!"

They walked back to the barn with a very tired Lucky behind them and Jacobus said, "Please stay for dinner and spend the night. Put your horses in the barn. We can start again early in the morning."

Will smiled. "After our little adventure out there today, we'll take you up on that Jacobus."

That night, in the kitchen after dinner, Jacobus and Sarah brought out a bottle and four glasses. Miles joked, "A little of the brown water perhaps?"

Jacobus laid out the glasses on the kitchen counter. "Yes, it's not cognac, but this is a good bourbon whisky that will do in a pinch." After he poured the glasses full, Jacobus raised his. "Will, I know I was a little hard on you out there today, but here's to old friends."

Will took a sip. "Jacobus, best friends are always keeping things interesting. There will be plenty of times, hopefully very soon, where I'll be able to get you back."

Sarah frowned and rolled her eyes. Jacobus placed his drink on the counter. "What do you mean? We haven't seen you before today in almost two years."

"Jacobus, we're here for more than just one horse. We want to travel west, and we want you to come with us."

"West!" Jacobus said in a loud voice.

"Yes, west! We want you and Sarah to come with us to California."

Jacobus reached for his drink and took a large sip. "Will, what in the world are you talking about? Our lives are here."

"That's what I used to think, but we have an opportunity to make large land purchases out there. So, we're inviting our best friends to travel with us and start a new community." He went on for several minutes telling Sarah and Jacobus the details of the plan and who they had invited. Will answered several questions Jacobus asked about Michel and getting past Indian Territory. After that, Sarah glanced at Jacobus and said, "Will, thank you, but Jacobus and I are going to need to have a little talk about this."

Jacobus set his glass down and leaned forward with his hands on the kitchen counter. "A *little* talk?" Then he looked back at Will and said "Are you crazy? My life has been spent here breeding and training horses Will. How are we going to do *all this* – out there?"

"No I'm not crazy. They've been racing horses on the ranches out there in a river valley where we're going."

"But I don't know a soul out there and they don't know me."

Will set his drink down and raised both of his arms. "A big reason we are going with a close knit group of people is to take care of each other."

"I'm only a horseman, Will. I have to be able to contribute."

"When we move, we don't leave our skills behind. We take them with us, Jacobus. Besides, selling your property here will allow you to buy five times its size out there."

They continued the conversation. More questions were asked than Will could completely answer and Jacobus said, "This would be a life changing experience with many risks – that is – if we live through the journey getting there."

"There are risks in everything we do already. I'm saying we will still be doing the same things – only out there. We only live once."

The next morning, Jacobus, Will and Miles ate a quick breakfast and went to the stable. Lucky was eating hay and neighing at Millie and Chipper because they were new to the barn.

Will suggested, "Why don't we try the saddle today?"

"You're just like the others. If I had known you wanted to saddle him, I would have had the doctor present."

"Very funny Jacobus, but I want to try."

"I'll say it again–"

"I know – it's my neck."

Will fastened a halter on Lucky and walked him out of his stall to the cross ties. Jacobus picked up Millie's saddle. "I'll get this on him if you'll grab the bridle and lunge line Will."

Cool breezes continued to sweep through the creek pastures as they walked back to the large pen. Lucky felt the wind, snorted and neighed loudly. Will tried to draw him closer by looping some of the extra line, but Lucky wanted to lead, so he maneuvered his body to face Will and pulled.

Miles helped Will with the line until Lucky calmed down and said, "This morning isn't going to be any good. That horse is *fresh* with this weather."

Jacobus patted Lucky in an effort to calm him down. "I hate to say it Will, but Miles may be right. You can still back out if you like."

"When was the last time you ever listened to Miles about anything Jacobus? The both of you can just shut up because I'm riding this horse – *fresh* or not."

"Will, I only meant–"

"Miles, apparently we've said enough. He's made up his mind. Let's see if he can do it. We're here anyway. Get the gate for him."

Then, after thirty minutes of lunging Lucky again, Will announced, "It's time. Let's bridle him." Will gave Lucky another carrot and stroked the mane above his eyes, then bridled him without much difficulty.

Miles shouted from outside the pen. "The girth Will!"

"It looks okay Miles." Then Will took a deep breath and held the reins against the saddle horn.

Jacobus, yelled, "He'll try to slide left when you get on, so watch out!"

Will pulled his hat down tight on his head, nodded at Jacobus and placed his foot in the left stirrup. He pulled himself up, but as he was swinging his right leg over the back of the saddle, Lucky jumped left and stopped. This move prevented Will from getting his right foot in the stirrup because all his weight was moving left. Then Lucky put his head down and started to buck. Will held on tight with his thighs because only the toe of his left boot was in a stirrup. Lucky kept bucking. Will was able to stay in the saddle and somehow got his right foot on the stirrup. He was even able to pull Lucky's head up with the reins. Lucky now had to go forward and didn't buck quite as much.

Jacobus yelled, "Ride him Will! Ride him!"

Miles shouted, "Go, Will, go! Show him who's boss!" Just when Will looked like he was going to be able to ride him, Lucky reared straight up. Will's face was pointed at the sky. Then Lucky stomped his front hoofs hard on the ground – put his head down again, and kicked his hind quarters and rear legs high. Will's rear end came out of the saddle. Lucky felt the separation and knew he was getting this person off his back just like all the others. He only had to make one more turn and would be free of another rider. Suddenly Will was thrown forward in the direction he was traveling before Lucky abruptly turned. Will made a valiant attempt not to fall, but ended up only holding onto the saddle horn with one hand and both feet out of the stirrups. Lucky knew it was over. His last move would be to simply dislodge Will, so he ran forward for a split second and suddenly stopped. Will's hand came off the saddle horn and he fell forward onto his back. The impact with the ground knocked the breath out of him for a few seconds. With his back on the ground and eyes closed, Will thought, *I just lost a lot of money, and the horse too.*

Jacobus and Miles jumped into the pen and ran to Will. Their faces came together above his, so when Will opened his eyes, the sun was partially blocked by their silhouettes. Between their hats, however, he could see Lucky standing twenty feet away watching him.

Jacobus grinned and softly said, "You get back up on that horse and ride him right now because I'm keeping all your money. We're going to need it in California!"

Will was a little startled. *Jacobus is in my face delivering this news now?* He tried not to laugh and responded in the same quiet tone because Jacobus' face was still so close. "That's great Jacobus. You have a unique way of letting me know. There was a lot of give in that saddle. You gave me the ole' loose cinch job – didn't you?"

Jacobus laughed. "It didn't matter how tight it was because that horse was always going to lay you out like a pancake!"

"I almost had him."

"Not even close – he was actually easy on you today for some reason! Your desperate gyration to hang on right before you got dumped was one of the funniest things I have ever seen!"

Will shook his head slowly and chuckled. "Yeah he was toying with me alright."

Jacobus stood up and reached for Will's hand, "Come on – get serious! Ride him again! This time – don't' get too far out of the saddle and lean into his neck when he rears! Be calm, steady and in charge. That horse is very smart. He can sense weakness."

Will allowed Jacobus to pull him up. "I'm glad you and Sarah are coming. It's a long road, but it'll be worth it." Then he walked to Lucky, held his reins, and whispered in Lucky's ear, "Are you going to let me ride you today?"

Lucky still had not moved, so Will grabbed the saddle horn and hopped on, but as soon as Lucky felt Will on his back, he put his head down and bucked more violently than he had only a few minutes ago. Will thought, *I've got to anticipate what he's going to do.*

Jacobus yelled, "You're too stiff – relax a little!"

The back of the saddle hit Will again on his rear end before he shouted, "Relax? I'm just trying not to die!"

Miles laughed. "Yeah Will – try to relax up there!"

Will managed to yell back, "Shut up Miles!" right before Lucky suddenly ran from the middle of the rink to the part of the fence where Jacobus and Miles were leaning and a loud BANG occurred. Miles jumped back yelling "Owww! – shit that hurts!"

Jacobus laughed. "Guess you won't be resting your hands on the rails again?"

"That horse is crazy!"

"Just the opposite Miles. He obviously likes Will more than you!"

Will tried to regain control by pulling as hard as he could on the reins. He couldn't believe the energy this horse still had after running on the lunge line. Now he felt that Lucky could actually sense *him* tiring. Lucky made another trip around the pen bucking as hard as he could, then jumped completely off the ground and landed on his front hooves. Will was thrown forward and used both hands to grab the saddle horn – then quickly took the reins again.

Miles, now standing safely away from the fence said, "Jacobus, he looks like a weakened boxer about ready to lose."

"I think you're right. One more quick buck and turn and it will be over."

Then something changed. Every time it seemed that

Will would fall off, Lucky slowed his bucking and speed, but not a lot – just enough to give Will a little time to re- cover. After that, Lucky would try to throw him off again. Will thought, *It's all a game to him*, so he stopped pulling on the reins and Lucky immediately slowed to a walk. Then Will took one hand away from the reins – patted Lucky on the side of the neck and said. "Okay Lucky – you win. Let's just go for a ride."

Miles asked, "What just happened, Jacobus?"

Will said, "Open the gate."

Jacobus shouted, "I don't know what's going on with that horse right now Will."

"Open it now. I know what I'm doing."

Jacobus opened the gate. Will softly nudged Lucky with his heels. Lucky turned his head toward Jacobus and stared at him for a couple of seconds. Jacobus nodded and Lucky shook his head up and down. Will nudged him again and Lucky bolted into the open field of blue grass. In a split second, Will moved faster on a horse than he had ever moved in his life.

Miles said, "I can't believe it! Look at them go – and the way the sun shows off that horse's muscles!"

"And the dark mane too, Miles – the way it keeps hitting Will in the face!"

"The length of those strides are incredible!"

"I know Miles...he's hardly touching the ground...now come on! I think Will's running him toward the road. Let's get to the house!"

Will and Lucky streaked across a quarter mile of the field and reached the road to the house. Then he turned onto the road. As Lucky ran, the morning sun flickered through the trees onto Will's face. He had never experienced such joy. The smile on his face was contagious.

Sarah, from the front porch window inside the house, saw light flickering off a black horse and rider through the trees, so she walked outside. As they came closer, she saw Will's smile and his blond hair bouncing up and down. Then she noticed Jacobus and Miles running to the house hooting and hollering. She had not seen this much happiness at their home in years. Jacobus ran up on the porch – hugged her and said, "Sarah, something special happened here today with Will and Lucky. I think it was meant to be."

CHAPTER FOUR
THE COMMITMENT

Before they left the Hendrickson's, Will purchased a Percheron crossbred for Ian. The Hendrickson's used this giant gray gelding named Dutch for heavy work on their farm. As they headed home that next morning, Miles volunteered to "pony" Dutch back to George Town since Lucky had just been broken. After two hundred yards from the Hendrickson's farm, Miles gave a sharp tug on the lead rope attached to Dutch and another kick to Chipper to catch up to Will and Lucky. Once he got even with Will, he said, "I can't believe they sold you their best work horse and their prized stallion."

"It's not like Jacobus and Sarah will never see these horses again. We're all going to the same place and this horse wasn't cheap."

"Did you see the difference in them compared to when we arrived a couple of days ago?"

"I know Miles. We had to help them. They have a purpose again. They're even coming to my house on Saturday and bringing Millie back."

"Look at you now – sitting high and mighty on your new stallion while I'm the one towing this monster with my free arm."

"You should probably keep switching arms as best you can for the next few hours Miles. You don't want to cramp up."

Saturday afternoon came, and Will still had no idea

about how many people would be attending. Whoever did come, though, were going to be treated to a first-class barbeque. He spent the entire morning arranging the tables, tablecloths and chairs. Miles came over mid-morning to prepare the meat and grills.

Right after three o' clock, Miles went to Will's house and shouted, "Hey look at this!"

"What?"

"Come over here and see." Will walked to his porch and looked at the road entering his property. There were at least thirty people making their way up the road to his house on foot, on horseback and in wagons. Will saw they included most of the families from the courthouse earlier in the week including the Hinrichs and McConnells. In the back of the crowd, he also saw Sarah maneuvering their wagon and horses up the road with Jacobus beside her riding Millie. There were also several other farming families and other millworkers coming up the drive. He was happy to see that he knew or had met almost everybody.

As people filtered onto his property, Will said, "Welcome, I'm happy to see y'all here today. I know more people are still arriving, but please get some food, a bourbon or two and enjoy yourselves. There's tea over there too."

Everyone formed a line and helped themselves to a plate of barbeque and a drink. Will was so focused on getting everyone ready to hear his speech, that he didn't notice those still arriving. While escorting guests to the buffet table, he saw several of them turning their heads toward the road entering his property, then he moved to see what was happening. It was Nathaniel, Abagail and Caleb Hamilton climbing down from their wagon.

Will waved and shouted, "Nate, y'all come on up here!" Samson hopped off their wagon and sprinted through the crowd to Will who clapped his hands and said, "Come here Samson!" Samson wound his way through the crowd and flopped down in front of Will for a belly rub. Nate made it through the crowd and reached out his right hand, but Will held out both arms instead. They hugged each other. Will whispered in his ear, "You won't be sorry."

Nate pulled back to face him. "All right, but it better be good."

"I'll show you, but first get some food."

Abigail was right behind Nate. "We'll hear you out tonight and that's all I'm going say right now."

"Abigail, It's going to be a long haul, but you won't be sorry when we get there. I promise."

Caleb, who had been holding Abigail's hand reached his out to Will and said "Mr. Richards, are you taking us on an adventure?"

Will smiled at Nate and Abigail – then he looked down at Caleb, took his hand, and said, "Yes, young man. We are going on an adventure that you will never forget." Then Will tapped Nate on the shoulder. "Please – you and your family sit here with me."

After thirty minutes of his guests eating, talking and kidding each other, Will assumed it was time to get down to business. Then Clyde McConnell led a contingent of people up to the table for seconds.

Will quickly stood up. "Okay y'all – thanks for coming. I'm ready to get started. Please have a seat." Then he pointed a finger at Clyde and raised his voice. "That goes for you buffet busters over there too!"

From his chair at a table, Miles said, "I think he's talking about you, *rib-plate!*"

Clyde grabbed a large serving spoon, pointed it at Miles and yelled, "Aren't those black eyes and that *snot locker* of yours a little early for Halloween? I bet Joseph has an extra place for you over there at the *nose* of his table!"

Miles grinned and shouted back, "Why don't you go take a ride on that millstone of yours–"

Clyde laughed as he finished spooning more ribs and potatoes on his plate, then grabbed his drink and walked to Miles, who asked, "What are you going to do now – sit on me?"

"Yes I am." Then Clyde turned his rear end to Miles' face and lowered himself. Everyone gasped before Miles dove onto the floor, and wave of laughter went through the guests when they saw Miles looking up at Clyde.

Will stopped laughing long enough to shout, "Look, the *moveable* object just met the irresistible force and wound up wallowing on the ground!"

Miles didn't immediately try to get up because he was laughing too hard. He looked up at Clyde who was now sitting in his chair smiling and raising a glass to the crowd. Then Clyde reached down, handed Miles his drink and pulled him off the floor. Both men slapped each other on the back and downed their bourbon's while the rest of the guests continued to laugh.

Nate leaned over to Will. "Are they always like this?"

"This is actually kind of tame for them right now."

"That was insulting, Will."

"They don't mean it, Nate. They act like a bunch of eighth graders at times, but they do stick up for each other when it counts."

"Whatever you say. I just can't ever see myself acting like that."

Will rolled his eyes and said, "You might be surprised. You obviously haven't spent much time with Ian." Then Will stood up – waved his hands and shouted, "Okay okay

– there's plenty of time for fun later, but right now we have something serious to talk about."

Those that did not yet have a seat took one and began to listen.

"What we're planning here will better our lives. With some help, I've found a place for us to settle in Northern California."

The crowd started to talk, whisper and laugh again. No one had heard anything about a specific destination yet. California and Oregon were just far away imaginations to most Scott County residents. Most of the people there knew nothing about the American West other than un-confirmed stories and occasional newspaper articles of people traveling to those areas.

Will walked toward the middle of the group of tables. "I know. I felt the same way you all did when I made the decision. It's a hell of a long way away, but this isn't the first time a human migration like ours has happened. We're *almost* like the passengers on the *Mayflower* – moving for something better."

Clyde said, "The *Mayflower* Will? Come on!"

Will held up his hands. "Ok – not *entirely* the *Mayflower*! Theirs might have been an easier journey. That voyage was a little over two months. Ours will be about six months if we're lucky." The laughter stopped. "The length of their journey is kind of close to what ours will be in terms of distance, but they didn't have to walk, and we walk the whole way after we get off the last steamboat in West Port."

Clyde said, "Will, they had a tough time traveling on the *Mayflower*, too."

"Yes, about five of them died before they ever set foot ashore, and they were pretty much *cared for* on the ship the whole way and didn't have to climb over mountains and face Indian tribes."

"All right, Will, we know there are dangers and risks, but you're a smart guy. Why did you gather us here to plan this trip if you feel it's not worth it?"

"Clyde, I know we will reach Northern California, but it's going to take a lot of patience and a very large commitment from each and every one of you for this to work."

"Will, we are aware of the risks and are here to listen to you anyway. From the conversations I've had with most people here – we don't *really* have a lot of choice if we want a better life. Most of us can't compete with the plantation owners and their slaves."

Will glanced at Nate and said loudly, "I agree. The plantation owners have an artificial economy that rides the backs of other human beings. It's immoral, and it's not always going to exist, but there are plenty other reasons to leave. The title problems many of you have gone through aren't going to get any better whether Greeley is here or not. "Let me show you where we'll be going." He laid out a sketched map of Northern California together with a rough map of the northwest, then pointed at a river valley. "Right here is the place, and from what I've heard, there's no better place on this continent to grow our crops, build our homes and ranch."

Clyde asked, "What happens after West Port?"

"Here Clyde, this other map shows where Fort John or Fort Laramie, or whatever the hell they call it now, is located."

"It looks like it's in Indian Territory Will."

"That's what they call it – then further to the west is a big rock structure that we've got to reach before the Fourth of July. They *even* call that Independence Rock."

"Why do we have to reach it by the Fourth of July?"

"So we don't freeze to death in the mountains before we get to California." The crowd went completely silent. Will then held up two pieces of paper. "The first list here is meant to be copied by each of you. It contains necessities that each family or person will need to have on the trip. Just remember, we'll be taking steamboats to West Port, so we'll get most all the supplies there at the outfitters."

"What about the wagons?" asked Clyde.

"We'll take several wagons to the steamboat in Frankfort if the Kentucky river's up – if not – we leave from the Portland side of the canal at the falls."

Martin Clearman, a former steamboat hand, said, "There's no regular passenger line going to Frankfort – just smaller freight boats."

"I know, Martin – I'm hiring a smaller transient boat to get us to St. Louis."

"Well let's hope the Kentucky River's up because that's a long walk up to Louisville and Portland."

"I'm with you, Martin. Now, this second piece of paper is going to be the list of those people committing to the journey. So, weigh this decision carefully before you place your name on it because I need a firm headcount – any questions?" There was a brief moment of silence which was quickly broken when a little boy ran to his mother screaming that Sammy had hit him in the face.

Clyde stood. "I'm sorry, Will, I'll take care of this." Other parents whispered among themselves, *It's that McConnell boy again.*

Martin said, "I have a question. How did you find out where to go, and how are we going to buy land in Northern California? The last I heard, Mexico governed Northern California."

Will glanced at Miles before answering – then turned

back to Martin. "I've received a lot of information these past two years from my good friend who was a fur trapper in the northwest. He knows the territory and the Indian tribes very well and can communicate with them. He will be our guide." Then Will's voice became lower. "To purchase the land though...I think I might have to become a Mexican citizen and convert to Catholicism."

Another roar of laughter consumed the moment. Clyde slapped the table and shouted to be heard again. "You have to be kidding Will! Catholic? The way you cuss? Besides, when was the last time you went to church...*any* church?"

Will let the laughter go on for a little while longer. He was smiling now too and said, "You're right. I can't remember the last time I went to church, but I hope it's not too late to start."

Clyde raised his hand and stood again. "Will, hell...The Catholic bishop that *visited* out here didn't even like us. He thought we were too raucous – I think were his words."

Nate stood. "It's all right Will. *We* Catholics will help guide you. You're going to need it!"

Will raised his hands again. "Okay everybody – I deserve it. Hopefully the California Catholics will be a little more lenient. I don't know, but everyone that wants to come needs to settle their affairs before spring." After that, a line developed behind Will's second list. One after another most of the men and women signed their names, said their goodbyes and left.

After they were gone, Miles said, "That was quite a job, Will, the perfect mixture of authority and love. You almost brought a tear to my eye."

"All right, Miles – enough of the smart remarks. Someone has to lead these people. We need them to be prepared for this, and they're not near ready. Looking at this list, we'll probably have enough for maybe ten wagons. Some of these folks tonight just came for the free meal. Time will tell, but no matter what, we're going to be joining a larger wagon train until we split off to California."

The walk home was very different for the people who placed their names on the list. They had entered into a very uncertain commitment that would change their lives. There were, however, some that did not sign. One of those was Tyler Shankle, a skinny obsequious busboy from one of the local hotels. Now, in the dark, he made his way downtown. Once there, he tied his horse, wound his way to the back of a three-story structure and gave two sharp knocks on the back door. A man in a suit slowly opened the door and said, "Get in here. What took you so long!"

Tyler was surprised by the rough tone. "I got here as quick as I could. It was a long way."

"Come with me. They are waiting for you." Tyler was taken down a dimly lit corridor and up a staircase to the middle floor of the structure where there was a round oak table. Sitting at the table were several men with a single lamp illuminating their faces. He realized he was in danger because a pistol was resting on the table. The men around the lamp stared at Tyler.

One of them shouted, "Get over here and sit down!"

Tyler quickly complied. When he was seated, he glanced around the room. His eye caught the shadow of a large muscular man in dark clothing walking with a limp. The man rounded the table and stopped behind Tyler.

The man that told Tyler to sit down was seated directly across from him and said, "Look at me son."

Tyler feared the worst. No one knew he was here. The

person that contacted him at the hotel was one of the men sitting across the table. He suddenly realized that this man never gave his name. All Tyler remembered him saying was, *you will be well paid.*

The man behind him spoke. "Where are they going?"

Tyler looked down at the table. "California sir."

"When are they leaving?"

Tyler started to turn his head and said in a cracking voice, "The spring sir."

The man across the table raised his voice. "I told you to look at *me* when you speak!"

Tyler stared directly at the man across the table again and said, "I'm sorry. They will take wagons to steamers and then West Port."

"What are the names of the steamboat companies?" asked the man across the table.

"I don't know. Mr. Richards said he would be getting back to them with more details." Tyler heard the man behind him limp away. The man seated across from Tyler slid him a sealed manila envelope. "Take this. Leave now from the door you entered. Try not to be seen leaving this building and remember that you were never here and you do not know any of us."

Tyler said, "Yes sir" and left.

The strongman re-entered the room, limped back to the table, and sat in Tyler's chair. Now the lamp elucidated a broken nose, two black eyes and a frown from its occupant. The man that slid Tyler the envelope said, "Well Anton, now we know."

Anton Greeley, who was happy to take his weight off his injured foot, asked, "Will that boy keep his mouth shut?"

"Don't worry about him Anton," Riley Draggart said. "Our plans are so far away from here, it won't matter."

CHAPTER FIVE
SELLING OUT

Spring came early this year in George Town. White and pink dogwoods bloomed through their delicately spaced branches and began to catch everyone's eye. The abundance of these bright blooms throughout the county contrasted with the dark Kentucky bluegrass.

For some in George Town, however, the beginning of the spring season would not be enjoyed as it should. The Fenwick's, for example, were prominent members of society and split their time between Ohio and Kentucky. They owned one of the lots near the middle of George Town. It was a piece of land large enough for a spacious house and detached barn like their neighbor, Anton Greeley. James Fenwick was a real estate entrepreneur who occasionally worked in George Town, but most of his business remained in Ohio. As a result, he did not know many of the residents but liked the town's community and the other beautiful areas that were part of Scott County, especially the creek properties.

This spring night, James Fenwick put his young daughters to bed and fell asleep with his wife, Michele. Shortly after that, he smelled smoke, sat up in bed, and looked out of their bedroom window to see fire engulfing their barn behind the house. James shouted, "The horses!" and ran from their house. When James reached the barn, it was filled with smoke. Horses desperately kicked inside their stalls to get free. He took a deep breath and ran to the first stall to open the gate, then the next. Two horses bolted out before he reached the other stall; but as soon as he lifted the latch, the terrified horse inside hit the gate and knocked James backwards onto the ground.

Michele ran out of the house to the barn. Two horses almost hit her as they ran from the fire, but she didn't care. She screamed, "No James no! Get out! Get out!" When she reached the barn, she saw her husband crawling out on his hands and knees. He collapsed and started coughing violently. The two young daughters ran out of the house behind their mother yelling, "Daddy! Daddy!" The fire spread so quickly that the beams supporting the barn roof broke downward, and the roof collapsed. The sounds of wood cracking together with the bright flickering light of the fire filled the night sky. The remaining horses never made it out alive. Michele and the two girls hugged their father and cried.

Soon they heard various neighbors coming to them and asking if everyone was all right. The way the fire overtook the barn was not natural. The fire had a pattern in the way it started and continued to burn. Two places on opposite sides of the barn seemed to have burned first. It was obvious that the fire was intentionally started. One of the neighbors asked, "Who did this to you, James?"

James was able to sit up now, but continued to cough. "I don't know. I have no enemies here. We just got back from a long vacation up east. This week, all I have done is ask about the McConnell property at the courthouse that is up for auction. A man with a scar on his face overheard me and rudely told me that I should not be interested in that property. I told him to mind his own business."

Two days later, Will and Miles rode into town from the south. Will was still trying to come to grips with the fact that he would lead a lot of people from this community on an unequalled journey across the country in a few days. Many of those traveling had never even traveled outside of Kentucky. As they rode, Miles said, "I still can't believe that day you rode that horse for the first time, Will. The way he toyed with you, and right when we thought you were done, he let you ride down Jacobus' road!"

"Yeah, it was just incredible. We're going to be with Jacobus and Sarah over the next few months, so y'all will have plenty of time to reminisce. Now, how are we coming with those extra rifles?"

"Ian said we would have them by Friday with all the powder and balls we need. He's making sure they all fire."

"Great. He's finally helping. When do you think he changed his mind?"

"You were right a long time ago. He always wanted to come – big new horse or not. He wanted to keep us guessing."

"The rest of the families are ready?"

"Pretty much. How long will we be in West Port before we start heading west?"

"Hard to say. Some wagons will be ready, but they'll probably still be assembling more when we get there."

"Thank God you were able to charter steamboats from those owners."

"It wasn't cheap, Miles. We had some of the others chipping in money though. I don't know how else we would do it – you've heard the nightmares!" Will gestured with his right hand moving it up and down as he explained, "We had to be able to count on some sort of schedule with all these people and horses. If *we* didn't hire those boats ourselves, some of us could be stuck on the Mississippi or the Missouri and the rest would be waiting in West Port for God knows how long. Would've been a damned mess!"

"I know. I'm glad you were dealing with it and not me."

"It's impossible to plan every step of this trip. Something's going to happen. I'm only trying to get rid of as many problems as I can."

"Relax Will."

"I am relaxed. It'll all work out – at least most people have been able to sell their land."

"Did you hear what happened a couple of nights ago?"

"What?"

"Someone burned down the Fenwick's barn and killed some of their horses."

"James Fenwick?"

"Yes – it was arson. He inquired about buying the McConnell's place this past week and his barn was burned to the ground."

"Why in the world would someone go after Fenwick?"

"That's not all. Walt Samuels was at the Stirrup and Heel Tavern and overheard two people talking about Greeley wanting the McConnell place to combine with the Donaldson place that he just bought. He wants to build a huge mill there on the Elkhorn. They supposedly have a mill dam approved too."

That's bullshit Miles! Why didn't you tell me this sooner!"

"I just heard about it."

"This town isn't that big! How in the hell does he think he's going to get away with it?"

"I don't think Greeley cares. He actually might want people to know it's him behind all this. He's crazy."

"He was always going to be the high bidder on that

land! What he wants is to get properties dirt cheap by intimidating buyers like the Fenwick's."

"I thought everyone that was going west was selling out?"

"Miles, even though we are leaving, we're not going to let our friends get cheated like this if we can help it."

"How are we going to help? It's not our property."

"I'll take care of the auction. You are the *gentleman* in this town, not me. You know a judge, don't you?"

"A couple."

"Well, they need to understand what's going on."

Several days later, four men quietly waited in the opulent living room of Anton Greeley. They weren't talking much because they were not happy with the reason for this meeting. They were hired by Greeley to find and secure properties for his lawyers, but recently they were having to take care of Greeley's personal matters as well. No one wanted to deal with his personal matters because those could wind up placing them all in jail. Forty-five minutes later, Greeley decided to grace them with his presence. It was obvious that he had been drinking. He walked in the room – threw his coat on a chair – said "Hello boys" and walked to his well stocked bar. With his back to those gathered to see him, he poured a large glass of bourbon and said, "Anyone else?"

There were no takers, so Greeley calmly walked over to the long leather couch where they were sitting and bellowed in a deep voice, "So, is everything cinched up with the courts?"

"Yes, Anton," said Riley Draggart. "We have received assurances that the mill dam will be permitted. All that remains are the final reviews. We should be able to build the size mill you want, but we must have the McConnell property to make this work."

Greeley smiled, took another large sip of the bourbon, and pompously said, "Oh...I think we have the McConnell property pretty much sewn up, and this auction today isn't going to cost an arm and a leg either." Draggart looked down and did not respond. Greeley finished his first glass and strode to the bar for a second. As he poured he said, "So, next topic – the river adventure! I understand that all we *really* have is a washed up drunk and the old man?"

"Well not entirely Anton, we also have–"

Greeley cut Draggart off before he could say anything else and shouted, "What do you mean! Those are the only two in charge right? Am I missing something?" He didn't stop at the couch but instead continued to walk around the room, while at the same time, taking another large sip of his drink. The others in the room had witnessed this before. Greeley's favorite pastime, it seemed, was drinking heavily and yelling at them. He downed the remainder of the second drink and walked back to the bar to refill the glass again; and with his back to the others, said in a much lower voice "This is ridiculous." Then he completely erupted. "This plan would have to improve just to be *bad* goddamnit! Is this *really* the best any of you can do!"

The men that didn't want to be there in the first place were now worried that passersby outside the mansion would hear Greeley yelling. An awkward silence came over the room. After a few seconds, the only one that spoke was Draggart again. "Anton, I thought we discussed this a long time ago. Do you want to be a suspect here or not?"

Greeley knew Draggart was right, but that didn't matter because he didn't like Draggart questioning him, so he laid into him again. "Riley, I still don't see how this guy that you dug up – that hasn't been on a boat in years, and a doddering old man are going to accomplish any of this!"

Draggart was silent for a few moments. "Everything is already in place. It's too late now to cancel it, Anton."

"The *only* good thing about this plan is that incompetence will win out in the end! The drunk will end up killing them all anyway! Greeley slurred his speech badly now and spat as he yelled. "Ha! They'll be skewered by a snag, and their bodies will be scattered all over the Missouri River!" With that, Greeley emptied his glass again and attempted to set it down on the bar, but missed, then refocused and gently placed it down with both hands before performing an odd exaggerated bow saying, "Goodbye gentlemen...the auction awaits." Then he uncharacteristically chuckled and left weaving as he walked.

Will and Miles approached the center of town and saw the courthouse coming into view.

"Are they going to be here for it?" asked Miles.

"Clyde will be. I don't know about Gretchen. They're happy to be coming west with us, but they aren't optimistic about this sale. They didn't want to have to sell at an auction. They have a good piece of land. This auction is their last hope for a fair price. Look at this place, Miles. It's normally crowded."

"Greeley scared all the other buyers off. Does he suspect anything?"

"I don't think so. He deserves what he gets. He can go to hell for all I care. The real risk today is all mine."

"What do you mean?"

"I'm guaranteeing Clyde the difference if his property sells below market price. Right now, we're simply here to observe and hope for the best. I'll know when I hear the right price."

"Don't be too obvious, Will, or you'll end up buying the property yourself."

Everyone interested gathered at the courthouse steps for this real estate auction that had been publicly noticed in Scott County. Miles and Will remained on their horses just far enough away so they wouldn't be confused with any of the bidders. The property was described as a twenty-acre tract of fertile creek land. Charles Randolph, well known in the county as the auctioneer, took his place for all to see and shouted, "Okay – first up is the McConnell creek property! We are going to start the bidding at ..." Will heard the starting bid and said to Miles "We have a long way to go."

Randolph leaned over after his first price call and asked his assistant, "Where are the usual bidders for a property like this?"

George Crabtree, who usually assisted with the property list, said, "They didn't come out. I don't think they wanted to be bidding against Greeley."

"What?" Randolph said. "This is a free auction."

George shrugged.

Greeley was still weaving from the effects of the bourbon as he approached the auction and struggled to take the printed auction notice from his jacket. He didn't hear Randolph's description of the property, but assumed this was the one that he was interested in and raised his hand anyway. Randolph looked at Greeley and acknowledged his bid as the starting price. More people now were gathering around the courthouse steps, but no one else chose to raise their hand. After Greeley's bid, Randolph called for a higher price but, there were no takers. Greeley smiled and thought, *This is going to be easy*. Randolph yelled "Going once! Going twice!" Then, a gray-haired man wearing a tweed jacket and white buttoned down shirt raised a rolled-up newspaper to signal a higher bid. Greeley had never seen this man before and assumed he was a bidder from Lexington or possibly the Ohio area.

Miles leaned over to Will asked, "Where'd you find him?"

"He was the lead singer from the musical group playing at Pratter's Hotel."

Miles tried not to laugh and quietly said, "That's hilarious, Will. He looks so distinguished."

"Yes, I thought the tweed jacket and white shirt would be a nice touch."

Randolph raised the bid again. The gray-haired man raised his rolled-up newspaper accepting the higher price and Randolph acknowledged his bid by pointing at him.

Greeley looked at the grey haired man and immediately raised his hand too. Randolph turned to Greeley with a confused look on his face. Greely looked back at Randolph and yelled "What?"

Randolph glanced down at George Crabtree and whispered, "I don't think this Greeley fellow is all there."

"Yep, clarify the last bid so he doesn't screw up the auction today."

Greely saw Randolph and Crabtree talking, but all he could think about were Draggart's words – *We must have the McConnell property to make this work!*

Will and Miles saw all this from a distance on their horses and did their best to avoid laughing. "Will softly said, "What's he doing?"

"I don't know – something's wrong. He could be drunk. He keeps swaying."

Randolph announced loudly that the property was

still at the last price and he had not yet raised it. Then he yelled out the new price. Greeley quickly raised his hand again accepting the new price, which was now greater than the market price. Randolph asked the crowd for an even higher bid.

Miles leaned over. "Is that it, Will?"

Will smiled. "No, let's have some fun." The man in the tweed jacket subtly looked over at Will to see if he should stop bidding. Will shook his head, almost unnoticeably, and Randolph yelled after the last raised price, "Do I hear–"

Draggart thought Greeley should have been back already and was curious about what had happened at the auction. He walked to the area around the courthouse and heard people saying, *Someone's trying to outbid Greeley*! After hearing this, he walked faster and heard Randolph's voice raising the price to at least a third more than the property was worth. Draggart knew something was wrong and ran toward the crowd which was growing in size. Randolph raised the bid again. The man in the tweed jacket looked at Will to see if he should quit. Will slowly shook his head again and held up two fingers. Then the grey-haired man shouted an amount that was twice the property's appraised value.

As Draggart moved through the onlookers, he noticed the connection between Richards and the man in the tweed jacket, so he ran toward Greeley to stop him from bidding again. Randolph yelled, "Going once!" Greeley immediately raised his hand with a new bid. Randolph pointed to Greeley again acknowledging him as the high bidder, then he yelled out an even higher price. The man in the tweed jacket looked at Will, who subtly nodded *yes* that it was over. The experienced Randolph saw Will's nod and could have taken that as a bid, so he yelled out to the crowd asking for any other bids higher than Greeley's. Draggart forced his way through the people yelling, "Anton – Anton! All he could hear now, though, was Randolph's final warning that he was closing the bidding "Going once! Going twice…! I'm going to sell it!" Then down came the gavel with a bang and Randolph yelled, "Sold to Anton Greeley!"

Draggart finally reached Greeley who slurred his speech saying, "I got it Riley! I got it!"

Riley grabbed Greeley by the lapels of his jacket. "You're drunk! The guy in the tweed jacket is Richard's shill! You paid double what the property was *even* worth!"

"Richards? Where?"

"Over there, Anton!" He pointed at Will who slowly tipped his hat, smiled at Greeley, turned Lucky and walked away with Miles and Chipper. "He ran the bidding up on you, Anton, and you paid it!"

Greeley sobered up at that moment. He looked around the crowd for the man in the tweed jacket and white shirt, but he had disappeared. Greeley dropped his auction program on the ground and stood in silence as everyone else walked away.

The next day at noon, a skinny but well-dressed, young man with wire rimmed oval glasses knocked on the door of Greeley's office residence. Draggart happened to be in the office working on Greeley's books. He stood up from his desk and answered the door. The young man said, "Hello, I work with Sage Reynolds on land acquisitions. He asked me to meet with Mr. Greeley to discuss the mill dam matter."

"Oh yes – of course, please come in. My name is Riley Draggart. I work with Anton Greeley. I do his accounting."

"Is Anton in?"

Draggart thought, *The kid's never met Anton Greeley but was now calling him by his first name?* Draggart smiled. "Why yes, *Anton* does happen to be in. May I take you to him?"

"Yes, we have business to discuss."

After the episode yesterday afternoon, Draggart wasn't going approach Greeley today for anything. Nevertheless, he took the young attorney up the steep staircase. After reaching the second story, Draggart said, "Anton, one of your attorneys is here!"

Greeley yelled, "What?"

Draggart said, "He is right in there." Then he turned around and went back downstairs as quickly as he could.

When the young attorney walked into the room, he was impressed by the furniture, rug, desk and artwork. Greeley was able to sleep off some effects of the alcohol he consumed yesterday, but was in no mood for problems. He walked into the room yelling, "What Riley? I didn't hear you!" Then he saw the skinny young stranger in a suit standing in the entryway. "Who are you, and how did you get in here?"

"Hello Anton, I am Geoffrey Shimwell. As your attorney, I have been working on the mill dam petition with the court."

Greeley thought, *This skinny little pencil neck in a suit and glasses is actually calling me by my first name?* Greeley, however, tried to remain calm. "So Sage sent you?"

"Yes, Anton, I am here to discuss..."

"Whatever you have to say had better be important." Greeley gestured to one of the chairs in front of his desk. Geoffrey sat, and Greeley walked behind the desk, leaned back in his leather chair, glanced up at the ceiling, took a deep breath, and said almost nicely, "Do you go by Geoff or Jeff?"

"No my name is Geoffrey."

Greeley could see this was going to be a very short conversation. "Geoffrey, why are you here?"

"Anton, I have been exclusively working on your mill dam issue with the court. Unfortunately, the court has denied your application for a mill dam on Elkhorn Creek despite all the elements necessary for a dam in this community having been met. Anton, what I need to also say is–"

"Stop!" said Greeley, who was about to throw the lawyer out of his office.

Geoffrey raised his hand. "Wait Anton. Sage simply wanted me to come in person to let you know that even though this was not the result you wanted, nothing is guaranteed with the law. We are only required to use our best efforts to–"

Greeley, with a louder voice, said, "I just paid double what the property was worth last night because your law firm assured Draggart that the mill dam would be approved!"

"Yes but sometimes that is just not the nature of the law, Anton. We don't know exactly what the judge relied on to base his decision for–"

"The *nature* of the law?"

"Yes, Anton legal precedents sometimes–"

"Geoffrey, you stop right there. This has not been a good couple of days and–"

"Anton, I would like you to consider–"

Greeley thought, *Now I see why Sage sent this little gnat over here.* Then he stood, walked around to the front of the desk, sat on the corner in front of Geoffrey, leaned over to him, and asked, "So, you had exclusive control of my case?"

"Yes and I just want to say that–"

"Geoffrey, how long have you been here in George Town – do you have any family here?"

"Why no – my family is all up East. I came here a couple of months ago because I loved the area and wanted to find place to settle down."

Greeley smiled. "Geoffrey, why don't we just forget about this. Sometimes things just don't work out. Please tell Sage what I said, and...here I will show you out." Then Greeley stood up and gestured toward the doorway to the stairs where Geoffrey had entered.

"Thank you Anton. I wish all our clients could be this understanding when things don't go their way."

When they reached the staircase. Greeley said, "Watch your step now."

"Thanks Anton, I think I've got this."

Greeley quietly whispered, "No, I don't think you do." Then Greeley grabbed Geoffrey by the back of his collar and belt, lifted him off the ground, and threw him head first down the stairs. Geoffrey screamed when he realized what was happening. Draggart heard the scream and the loud *bangs* that followed. Greeley shouted in a loud voice from the top of the staircase. "Riley, I think Geoffrey missed a step. Is he okay?"

Riley moved to the stairwell – looked at the dead body at the bottom and yelled back, "No Anton, I think you've lost this lawyer."

Greeley shouted back, "It's all right, we have more. Go tell Sage and the authorities that there has been a terrible accident here today."

CHAPTER SIX
THE FLOOD

Katherine Hinrichs yelled, "Come on! We have to go! That boat's not going to wait!"

"Katherine, we know," said her mother, Elizabeth.

Joseph Hinrichs looked out their front window and shouted, "He's here! Come on! The wagon's here! Let's go!" Katherine tried to drag her trunk toward the front door.

Joseph said, "Here Katherine I've got it – where's your mother gone to?"

Randall Mabry met Joseph at the doorway. "Hey Joseph, today's the big day, right!"

"Yep, moving day is finally here. We appreciate the ride to Frankfort, Randy. We couldn't do it without you. Prepare yourself for the 'When are we going to be there?' questions from Katherine after about a mile or so."

"Three trunks, Joseph?"

Joseph thought about his question. The three trunks amounted to the sum total of all they would take with them from their lives in Kentucky. Joseph quickly looked down because he didn't want Randall to see him shed tears in front of his family. Then he said, "Yes, three trunks. That's it."

Other farmers like Randall Mabry were not going to California but wanted to help their friends and neighbors travel to the steamboat in Frankfort about eighteen miles to the west. Randall helped Joseph, Elizabeth and Katherine place their trunks on his long flatbed wagon.

Joseph saw Elizabeth was about to cry. He hugged her. "I know, I know."

Katherine saw her face. "It's okay, Mommy. This is going to be great."

Will traveled to Great Crossings, a community west of Georgetown where everyone would be meeting. He saw Miles hunched over his saddle horn with a disgruntled look on his face and shouted "Miles, you look like you're about to throw up."

Miles somberly said, "No I'm fine. I guess we have only around three thousand miles to go now."

Will laughed. "More or less I suppose. Look – you're *going* to make it – just think of one day at a time – besides we're on a boat for about a third of it anyway."

Miles' face changed to a familiar worried stare. "Don't remind me."

"We're arranging for you to help work the boilers so you can make sure everything goes smoothly. I hope you brought some light clothing. I hear that it gets pretty hot down there."

Miles grimaced. "I would rather be towed behind the boat in a canoe all the way to West Port than ride on that floating bomb."

"That, or you could stretch a hammock across the bow and hang there for everyone to see. Hey look! Here they come."

Miles turned his head and saw Nate riding Dominick with Abigail, Caleb and Samson on one of the many wagons transporting everyone, except for those riding horses and walking. Will looked at Ian's beard, rifle, flapping long dark jacket and his big horse, then he shouted loudly, "Look Miles, if it isn't *William Wallace* on his way to the Battle of Stirling Bridge!"

Ian left the front of the wagons, rode back and said, "That was the bravest Will, I've ever heard of. You've got a lot of room for improvement, jackass!"

Will slowly raised his right hand above his head and lowered it away in an exaggerated sweeping gesture. "Welcome Ian! We're glad you decided to come after all!"

Ian pulled along side of Will and Lucky. "Did you and Miles bring your little swords so you can play soldier on our trip?"

Will smiled. "Yes they're tied to our trunks on that last wagon. We loaded them yesterday. Do you want to play, too, when we get a chance?"

Dutch didn't want to be close to Chipper. He jumped slightly to the left before Ian controlled him. "Don't think I'm not humoring you boys, too. I appreciate the horse here, Will, but a gift is a gift. I owe you nothing. *I'll* see how things go up to West Port. That's when I decide to come back to Kentucky or not." Then Ian kicked Dutch and cantered him back to the front of the wagons.

Miles started to speak, but Will put up his hand. "Miles, let it go. He'll be saying that kind of thing until we cross the Sierras."

Most people walked because the wagons were loaded with trunks and the ride was very bumpy and uncomfortable. Many of the men and women, however, took turns riding horses because they were bringing so many. Jacobus brought four. Clyde McConnell had five and was riding his favorite, a big athletic gelding named Mirage who had a habit of moving his head up and down and rearing on his hind legs. His problem now was overstimulation from all the other horses and people, so the other riders gave Mirage as much room as they could.

They traveled for a few more miles west and camped for the night. The next day after breakfast, they set out for Frankfort. After they had traveled about half of the way, it began to rain and everyone seemed to slow down. Miles said, "Will, are we going to make it to Frankfort by nightfall at this rate?"

"You're right. We need to pick it up a notch. Go over to–"

Before Miles could answer, they heard Ian behind them shouting. "We'll never make it walking like your grandparents! Pick up the pace, you sissies! There'll be plenty of time to rest on the boat!" Ian continued all the way to the front. The men driving the horse teams on the wagons slapped the reins on their backs. The horses popped their heads up and looked around. Some began to neigh loudly, but they all started to walk faster.

Will said quietly to Miles, "I knew it was a good idea to get that old fart to come with us. Look at him actually working out there! We may actually have a team."

"I know – It really means something now. They want it."

When they reached the outskirts of Frankfort, the rain stopped, and the sky had mostly cleared except for a few light clouds. They approached a high point before they would begin the walk down to the landing.

Katherine yelled, "Look there's smoke!"

Joseph said, "That's the boat, Katherine!"

The sun was setting while the boat made its way to the landing. Points of light issued from several places on its three decks. All the activity from the crew made the lights flicker in the distance. It looked like a giant rectangular wedding cake on a plate moving toward them across the water. What caught everyone's attention though was the sheer amount of black smoke coming from the dark stacks. Since there was not much of a breeze, the smoke lingered in the area and darkened the sky.

A tall clean-shaven man with graying hair protruding from under his black captain's hat stood on the hurricane deck. Gunny, the first mate, came to him and said, "Uncle Lane, I almost forgot to ask you back in Louisville if you were coming to the house when we get back from St. Louis?"

Captain Bridges frowned. "Not so loud...I'm 'Captain' when we're on the boat Jim – but tell my sister yes, I will be there."

"Sorry *Captain*. Who are we picking up this time?"

"Some rich rancher and God only knows who else. The rancher met with one of our owners and chartered the entire boat to St. Louis for his passengers alone."

"Sounds like they want to stay together as much as possible. I bet they're going to Missouri."

"Great – a bunch of slow-moving farmers and ranchers we are going to take forever to get aboard! Well they've got another thing coming because we're going to beat that rain up north if it kills me."

"Aye Captain. We'll turn her around quickly."

"I mean it, Gunny. Don't take any lip. Tell Titus and Trey the same!" Captain Bridges saw movement taking place on the hill and yelled, "There they are! Let's let them know we're here!" A loud bell sounded, as the boat made its way to the landing. Everyone seated on the wagons quickly stood to get a better view. The children heard the bell and started to walk faster and faster toward the steamboat.

From the middle of the line of people and wagon's, Sammy McConnell looked at Katherine. "I bet I can beat you down there."

Katherine saw Sammy's baggy pants and ran toward the boat shouting, "Not me you won't!" Sammy ran as fast as he could, but wasn't catching her, so he tried desperately to run faster.

Other children, except for Caleb, followed their lead and raced down to the steamboat. Nate and Abigail were quick to keep him in their wagon. The other parents, however, could only scream "Slow down!" The children either didn't hear or didn't care because they continued running to the river bank.

Clyde McConnell was walking with Gretchen holding Mirage's reins. He saw what was happening, gave the reins to Gretchen, and began running too because he knew Sammy wouldn't stop. Sammy had almost reached Katherine at the water's edge when he tried to make up the distance by leaning forward. He was just a couple of steps behind her, but he leaned too much and started to fall. Each step now was an attempt to regain his balance. Katherine stopped right at the water's edge, and Sammy tumbled into the Kentucky River. Then he splashed, as if he were fighting something under the water.

Half a second later, the stopping bell of the steamboat sounded. The engineer immediately closed the throttle valve and stopped the engines. Then the backing bell rang and the paddle wheel spun slowly in reverse. Drew Smithwood, the engineer, shouted into his speaking tube "What is it, Peerless?"

The response came quickly. "Kid in the water, Smitty, keep backing her up!" said the boat's pilot.

Captain Bridges saw what happened as well. He thought, *not again* and yelled to his crew, "Kid in the water! Larboard side! Go now!" Crewmen dropped the ropes they were holding, ran to the left side of the boat and dove into the river. They all swam hard because Sammy had just disappeared under the water. The water around the riverbank was deeper and moving a little faster than usual because of the rain. Clyde panicked. He saw that Sammy had not come up. He came across an uneven area, then tripped and fell skinning his face on the ground, but popped back up and kept running. Gretchen gave Mirage's reins to a friend and screamed hysterically, "Sammy! Sammy!" as she ran down the hill.

Gunny, the first mate, beat everyone else to the area where Sammy was last seen. He swam down at the point where Katherine was gesturing. Everyone on shore was silent. Gunny came up with Sammy after a few seconds.

Katherine yelled, "He got him! He got him!"

Gunny swam to the river bank with only one arm while he held Sammy's face up with the other. Once he was up on the bank, Gunny leaned Sammy over his knee and slapped him on the back. Sammy soon coughed up river water.

Gunny saw the adults coming down the hill and said, "He's swallowed some water, but he's going to be all right!"

When Clyde finally reached Sammy. He was completely overcome and knelt crying, then put his arm around Sammy. "What happened son?" Sammy sat up and coughed violently. Gunny stood with his wet clothes sticking to his muscular physique. Everyone could see the young man that saved Sammy was an athlete.

Gunny pushed the dark wet hair out of his face and said, "His pants were stuck on a big log branch down there. I was lucky to get him out of the pants." Then Gunny pointed to Clyde's face. "You're bleeding sir."

Clyde cut several places on his face when he tumbled down the hill. He gently patted Sammy on the back. "I don't care. You saved my son's life! What is your name?"

"Jim Gunther sir, first mate of the *Cypress Queen*."

Will and Miles had been at the front of the line when the children started running. As soon as he saw what was happening behind him, he and Miles maneuvered their horses back quickly to the water's edge and shouted back at the others that were still arriving on the scene. "He's all right! Sammy's Okay!" Then, Will took off his hat, ran his fingers through his hair, sat back in the saddle and sighed. "We were very fortunate here today, Miles. That kid almost died."

"I know, and we haven't even gotten to the landing yet." Miles looked at all the people surrounding Sammy. "You and I obviously don't *really* know what it's like traveling with kids do we?"

"We'll fix that, Miles. First let's meet the captain, see how quickly that boat unloads its freight, then get the kids and parents aboard."

Miles looked at the people talking to the McConnell's and frowned. "The kids on the boat will be contained, but they can still fall off..."

"The boat Miles! I think the captain's yelling at the guys over there who saved Sammy. He wants them to meet him over at the landing – come on!"

At the landing, the crew swiveled a gangplank from the front of the boat to the dock.

The captain quickly walked off the boat and extended his hand. "I'm Lane Bridges."

Will shook his rough hand. "Will Richards, Captain. Thank you for saving the boy that got away from us."

The captain did not respond kindly "That was not good, Will. We got lucky. It goes the other way some-times."

Will could tell the captain was angry, but before he could answer, the crew rushed past them carrying freight off the boat. Two crew members carrying a large wooden crate accidentally bumped Miles in the back, and set the crate down on the landing.

Nate and Abigail walked aboard with Caleb and Samson on a leash. Abigail leaned over to Will and said, "Why is he so upset?"

"I don't know. Maybe he's having a bad day."

Captain Bridges had a schedule to keep. He held a checklist in his hand for everything being unloaded and the people that had to pay for its transportation and spoke curtly, "Will, I can talk to you more when we get underway. The moon is out right now, and the river is up. I have to get down the Ohio ahead of the run-off before it starts raining again." He gestured to an open area of land next to the landing. "You get your horses and whatever else you have ready to board over there." Then he looked over Miles' shoulder and began shouting orders. "Did you not hear me on deck? Get the wood on board at the same time! Move it!" Will's face was expressionless. He thought, *This is how our captain greets his paying passengers?*

Miles said, "Look Will, it's our only ride. We only have to put up with this guy to St. Louis."

"Richards!" shouted the captain. "Load the skittish horses last!"

Jacobus was leading one of their horses to the boat and whispered to Sarah, "He may be an ass, but he does know something about horses."

Will stepped back. "Let's tell Randy and the others goodbye, Miles. It's time to go."

After the boat left the landing, Captain Bridges saw the McConnell's at the bow. He introduced himself and knelt to where he could look Sammy in his eyes and said softly, "Young man, you gave us quite a scare out there today."

Sammy said, "I'm sorry."

"I know you are, Sammy. It's all right. Tell me, though, have you ever been on a steamboat before?"

"No sir."

"Would you like me to show you the pilothouse?"

"Yeah!"

Captain Bridges asked, "Will that be okay?"

Clyde looked at Gretchen and smiled. "You take your time, Captain."

"Good – I'll have him back in a little while. Sammy you're going to like this. Stay close to me now."

As they walked on the main deck, Sammy pointed at three crewmen stacking wood. "Who are they?"

"That's Michael, Titus and Rafael. They are some of the best crewmen I have."

Sammy pointed at the man that seemed to be in charge of the others helping load the boat. "Which one is he?"

"That's Titus. I have known him for many years. He is probably the strongest and most experienced man on here. If you ever need anything and can't find me or Gunny – you go to him."

"Where are we going now?"

"Well, we are on the main deck now. Follow me up these stairs to the boiler deck where you will be staying."

"With my mom and dad?"

"Usually these rooms are for women and children. The men stay with the animals on the main deck."

"So my father is sleeping with the horses?"

Yes, but our trip isn't long. Now let's go up to where Gunny and I stay."

"He's the one that saved me?"

"He sure did. We don't want that to happen again, so never go to the main deck without one of your parents. If you fell in the water with the boat moving, you could drown."

"I know."

"Good Sammy. You have a mother and father that love

you. Remember that."

"I will. I promise."

"All right, here we are at the top of the boat on the hurricane deck."

"Why do they call it the hurricane deck?"

Captain Bridges held Sammy's hand and thought, *He used to act like this – always with questions.* Now after seeing that Sammy was all right, he wanted to answer all the questions this little boy could ask. "A long time ago they started calling it that because it was windy on top of the boat."

Sammy nodded, then pointed. "What's that little house?"

"It's the pilothouse. There are two pilots, Peerless and Jamie. They take turns after a few hours, because we are running the boat all the time if we can."

"What's that sound?"

"That's the sound of the paddle wheel turning, Sammy. The paddle wheel propels the boat forward and back-ward. The paddles that hit the water are called buckets and..."

Will was on the main deck taking care of the horses and saw Sammy and the captain going to the top of the boat. Gunny was walking toward him carrying wood on his right shoulder. "Hey, I'm Will Richards – aren't you the man that saved Sammy today?"

"Yes sir – Jim Gunther – First Mate. They call me Gunny."

Will shook his hand. "That's kind of the captain to take Sammy up to the pilothouse."

"It's important to him, Will. Captain lost a son in a drowning accident when we were on another steamboat a few years ago. It still bothers him."

Will thought, *no wonder he was upset.*

Gunny placed the wood on the deck and looked down at the water running past them for a few seconds. "Captain shows us a brave front." Then Gunny looked up at Will with tears in his eyes. "He has a great wife and two more sons, but on days like today – you see how he still feels."

Will wondered if Gunny had tried to save the captain's son as he did with Sammy. "I understand. I also know watching our children is not your job and you can't spend time doing it."

"No we can't, but I saw Captain brushing you off at the landing and thought you should know. The captain really is a good guy."

"Wow!" was all Sammy could say as Captain Bridges held him up to the area where the pilots controlled the boat. "You can see a whole lot from up from here!"

"Yes Sammy. He can see everything. That's why the lights are off. Our eyes adjust to the dark – right Peerless?"

Peerless Hart, a man in his mid-twenties with light brown hair and strong features, looked at Sammy. "He's right young man, but I'm just one of the pilots. The other is Jamie. We take turns at the wheel – both day and night."

Sammy wrinkled his forehead. "Hey – I can't see everything so you can't either. How old are you?"

Peerless smiled. "No I can't see everything, but I have to know what it is that I *can't* see – and I'm twenty-six."

Captain Bridges placed his hand on Sammy's shoulder. "Peerless is very good at what he does. What he's trying to say is, that he knows this river just like he knows the road to his house in Louisville, even when it's dark." Then Captain Bridges pointed at an area of the river in front of them. "Why, he knows that bend in the river over there has a reef that you can't even see because the water is high now."

"He knows more than you, Captain Bridges?"

"Yes, even though he is much younger, he knows more than I do about the rivers we are traveling now. He is completely in charge of this boat when it is moving."

Sammy thought for a second. "He must make a lot of money!"

"Sometimes he makes more money than me, Sammy."

Sammy looked at both of them and glanced out at the river. "I want to be a pilot!"

Peerless looked back at Captain Bridges with a little smile.

The captain rolled his eyes and said laughing, "Sometimes I do, too, Sammy." He tapped Peerless' shoulder. "Sammy, you can be a pilot, *right now*! If that's all right, Peerless?"

Peerless knew this was coming and grabbed a tall stool. He placed it in front of the large pilot wheel. "Stand up here, young man! Let's see what you've got!"

Down on the main deck, Will saw Miles shoveling horse muck. "I had a visit with the first mate, Gunny."

"That's great, Will, I see him all the time now. He's actually working like me, buddy. Now pick up a shovel and help. We are sleeping down here remember?"

"Miles, he told me the captain lost a son in an accident just like today with Sammy. It happened when they were both on another boat together."

Miles stopped shoveling and placed a hand on his low back. "You never know what's going on in someone else's life. I'm glad we didn't argue with him back there."

Will grabbed another shovel. "Gunny also saw the captain being short with us before we boarded, but when he was talking I could tell there was something else going on. He said when he saw Sammy go in the water, 'He knew he had to save him.' I think he might have been the one that tried to save the captain's son."

"Could be. You getting tired yet? It's been a long day."

Will looked around and saw Nate standing next to Dominick. "Yeah – bet the others are ready to turn in too. Hey Nate, how are you guys?"

"Doing fine. I went up and gave Abby and Caleb a good night kiss and brought Samson down here to urinate and defecate like the rest of the animals, but even *he* turned his nose up at this mess and insisted that I take him back upstairs."

"Nate, we're only on these boats for a few days. You're going to be able to walk, eat and sleep with Abigail and Caleb every day after that."

"So you're saying it can't get any worse?"

Will looked Nate in the eye and said, "I don't see how," right before Dominick expelled half a gallon of urine onto the deck right behind him.

Gretchen was looking over her shoulder again while pretending to be listening to what Clyde was saying. "They've been gone for a long time."

Clyde took her hand. "Gretchen, I think it's okay. That boy is getting a good lesson up there, and I think he's going to listen more to the captain than he listens to us anyway."

"Yes – I suppose he's fine."

"I know you don't mean that, but he's with the captain and..." Then Clyde looked over his shoulder and nudged her. She turned and saw Captain Bridges walking toward them holding Sammy's hand.

Sammy wore a crewman's cap that was too large for him. He ran to her shouting, "Mommy – I piloted the boat! That was me steering back there!"

Captain Bridges smiled. "He handled the boat very well up there. He's a member of the crew now. We also talked about staying with our parents when we are on the deck."

Sammy looked his mother in the eye. "We can't have anyone fall off the boat, Mommy."

Captain Bridges said, "You all try to get some sleep now before we get to the Ohio. There will be a lot to see on that river in the morning."

Clyde gave Sammy a big hug. "All right, Captain, we'll see you in the morning." Then he gave Gretchen a kiss and walked to his sleeping area with the rest of the men on the main deck.

Gretchen watched Clyde walk away. "Sammy, let's go to bed." She took his hand and walked to the stairs leading to the boiler deck.

Gretchen placed her hand gently on the back of his head. "There were not enough rooms and beds for everyone, so daddy and the rest of the men are sleeping with the horses."

"I already knew that mommy."

The two pilots continued to take their turns at the wheel. Peerless was starting his night shift again when the captain came into the pilothouse. "Peerless I guess you saw it?"

"Storm up north – lot of lightning, Captain."

"The Ohio is already high, and I bet that storm's going to give us run-off at the Wabash River."

"It might, but we have plenty of wood now, Captain. We can keep running fast past the Wabash to get by the worst of it – if it starts to get bad – we just tie up to the bank and wait it out."

"Okay Peerless, but the second you see it moving too fast, get over."

"Aye aye, Captain."

Captain Bridges paused at door to the pilothouse before he left. "We still need to see better. I'm getting Gunny to get rid of all unnecessary lights and tarp the other areas."

After another three hours, Jamie Petty came into the pilothouse. "Peerless, go get some sleep. It'll be dawn soon."

"All right. We are pushing her to get past the Wabash river in case there's flooding from that storm. Smitty's going to want to back off, but we have to keep moving."

"Peerless I have..."

"There's going to be a lot of runoff. Watch the Ohio after you pass the Wabash too Jamie!"

"I have it, Peerless! Don't worry. Get some sleep."

Peerless stopped and looked out at the river one last time. He realized he was wound up. He wanted to stay, but there was nothing more he could do right now. He knew he needed sleep. "Ok, Jamie, I'm out – also, watch for debris."

Peerless went to his quarters on the hurricane deck. He was exhausted and fell asleep without taking off his uniform. All he could hear now were the sounds from the engine room, and the paddle wheel hitting the water.

In the morning, those on the starboard side of the boat could see the large open area of water where the Wabash River met with the Ohio. The presence of clouds made for a colorful sunrise. The Wabash was flowing faster than the Ohio, and bringing with it parts of its riverbank that had recently been ripped away by the high volume of water. The light brown color of the sediment rushing into the confluence from the Wabash expanded exponentially, though, and became the new color of the Ohio.

Jamie had been piloting the ship for a little over two

hours when Captain Bridges walked into the pilothouse. "Well it's here, Jamie. We didn't beat it."

"It's not the worst, Captain. No driftwood or other debris from the run-off yet. I can maneuver just fine. I feel water behind us, but we should be okay as long as we keep this speed."

"The river is rising, Jamie."

"I know, but we just can't tie up here, Captain, even if we wanted to. We have better places in a few miles."

Captain Bridges frowned, but before he went back down to the main deck, said, "I don't care, Jamie. Get us to the river bank as soon as you can. That's an order."

Gunny saw the Captain coming down the stairs. "Captain, we've been going pretty fast for a while now."

"I don't like it either, Gunny. We're going to tie up as soon as we can."

Will was awake with a coffee cup in his hand looking for a refill and saw Martin Clearman on the main deck. "Martin, beautiful morning! What do you think?"

Martin looked at the water and then pointed to what the crew was doing. "We're too late. We should have tied up and waited the flood out before we got to the Wabash."

"What do you mean?"

"This sternwheeler, Will, is made for going upstream in shallow water. Not trying to out run the current on a fast river."

TWEET. Jamie jumped when he heard the signal from the speaking tube in the engine room. He took a moment to regain his composure and answered. "What is it Smitty?"

Smitty wiped sweat from his face and shouted, "What do you mean what is it? You unmitigated greenhorn! You know we can't keep this speed up. Do you want to come down here and look at the gauge? You're going to have to make a decision!"

Jamie thought for a second. "We're tying up as soon as we can. Get us around the next bend."

"No – you get us off this river, Jamie."

Jamie was not as calm as he was when he started his shift. He knew he had to find a way to stop the boat, but the river current had become much faster. If he did not keep the speed of the boat faster than the current, it would be pushed from behind and spin out of control. He had been alone at the wheel for a long time, and now began to worry about his ability to safely stop the boat. He kept glancing at the water by the shore hoping to find a place to tie up, but he only saw steep rock formations on the river's north side. With his eyes searching the river bank, he failed to see the large dark object in the water that had moved in front of the bow. He thought again, *Where is Peerless? It has to be time for him to take over.*

CHAPTER SEVEN
OUT OF CONTROL

*B*ANG. Everyone on board felt something large hit the bottom of the hull. As the boat passed over it, the object made a raking sound that vibrated the hull from bow to stern. Peerless opened his eyes. He knew immediately what had happened and tried to get to the pilothouse as fast as he could. Before he could get there, though, he heard the cracking and clattering sound of something hitting the paddle wheel. As he came into the pilothouse, Jamie's back was to him. He was frantically trying to regain control of the boat.

"Give it to me Jamie. You're done. Go see how bad it is."

When Jamie started to the door, Captain Bridges burst into the pilothouse. "Most of the buckets on the right side of the wheel are damaged. What happened!"

Peerless looked at Jamie. "We don't know yet – probably part of a tree." The boat's stern slid to the right in the current. Peerless turned into the direction of the slide. "We still have some rudder," he yelled into the tube. "Smitty! All you have – now!"

Smitty shouted back, "Peerless – we're already running too hot. If I give you more it could blow."

"You heard me, Smitty. All you've got – now! I am not losing this boat!"

Captain Bridges knew he couldn't do any more in the pilothouse. "Do your best to get us to the riverbank. I'm going to the passengers."

The paddle wheel began to spin at a much faster rate because one third of the buckets that normally contact the water were gone. The crew in the engine room burned wood and raised steam in the boilers as quickly as they could, but it was still not enough to control the boat. On his way down to the boiler deck, Captain Bridges saw Gretchen and Sarah.

"What's happening!" Gretchen cried.

"Both of you – get to your rooms quickly and stay there! Tell the others to do the same." Gretchen's lip quivered. Captain Bridges placed his hand on her shoulder and firmly said, "I'm sorry, but we are in danger. Do as I say now." As soon as he spoke, he heard Samson in Abigail and Caleb's room howling. He shook his head and continued down the stairs to the main deck.

Gunny ran by him shouting, "All passengers to the middle of the boat now!" Then Gunny looked at the Captain. "We've lost control haven't we?"

"Yes – keep doing everything you can to protect the passengers."

Peerless shouted into the speaking tube again, "Smitty! Back her off a bit – let her drift – let the current take her." Then he suddenly felt less control in the pilot wheel and looked back at Jamie, who still stood a few feet away from him with a blank stare on his face. "Stop feeling sorry for yourself, Jamie! Get to the stern and see what's happened to the rudders!" Jamie ran out of the pilothouse to the back of the hurricane deck. Peerless slowly used the boats' power, in spurts, to regain control as they moved closer to the river bank. "Smitty – again now! We've got to straighten her out again."

"The pressure gauge is still too high!"

"Damn the gauge! Do it now!" Peerless positioned the bow of the boat so that it was moving at an angle toward the riverbank. "Stay with me Smitty – half of what you've got now. We're still too fast to run her up." Back on the main deck, there was furious movement by a few crew members who were preparing to jump off the boat and tie the ropes to anything they could find.

On the north bank of the river, a man named Shamus Little was baiting a fishing hook and said to his brother Ray, "That steamboat's in trouble. Go get the boys."

Ray Little smiled and walked a few yards behind trees that were close to the river and yelled, "Hey, steamboat's in trouble. Load the guns and get over here now!"

Two minutes later, several unshaven men in ratty clothes appeared next to the Little brothers with rifles. "Where do you think they'll tie it?" asked one of them.

Shamus said, "Right here. It can only be that stretch with no rocks, but they're too fast now."

The frantic activity on the boat upset the horses. The ones closest to the outside began to kick out and pull on ties clipped to their halters. Mirage was the worst. He was already skittish, but the noise and activity made him even more upset. He thrashed back and forth and neighed loudly. Clyde was at Mirage's nose trying to prevent him from rearing, but it wasn't working. Jacobus left his horses to help. Gunny heard the commotion and started running from the bow toward the starboard side railings on the main deck. Mirage reared up, pulled the cross ties loose, and ran toward the bow. Gunny grabbed one of the broken ties, but it was too late. Mirage's back legs slipped, and he slid toward the edge. Then the boat made a sudden jerk when the paddle wheel started again, and Mirage's hind legs came off the deck. Titus and Rafael were nearby and tried to save Gunny, but Mirage was too heavy once he started to fall. Mirage and Gunny splashed into the river. They were both under water for a couple of seconds, but as soon as they came up, they were caught in the main current and taken quickly away from the boat.

Captain Bridges saw what had happened and yelled "Gunny!" Titus started to take off his boots, but Captain Bridges held up his hand. "No Titus, you're not going to try it. We will not be losing you, too. The current is too strong."

Gunny and Mirage bobbed in the fast water ahead of the boat, which kept moving further off the main stream to the river bank. Gunny looked to still be holding onto a tie because his head kept coming up and down behind Mirage's head. Captain Bridges' face showed no emotion other than a twitch on his cheek.

Will was in the middle of all the other horses when Gunny fell in. When he made it to the Captain, he said "He's a great swimmer. We will get him back." Captain Bridges did not respond. His face remained staring at the place where he last saw Gunny.

The *Cypress Queen* pointed toward the riverbank allowing the Little's to see the Larboard side and the activity in and around the main deck. "Did you see that Shamus?" said Ray. "There's a man and a horse in the water going down stream!"

Shamus pointed at three of the ratty bunch of men. "Get over to the other fishing place by the road now! Get that horse, and that guy if they're still alive and take 'em to the house. We'll meet you later!" The three men closest to Shamus stood up and went to their horses. Shamus looked back at Ray. "That sized steamboat's not on a regular trade route with that many horses. Those people are moving."

Ray smiled. "This is our day! If they're moving, you know they got money with 'em too."

Jamie hurried back to door of the pilothouse. "Peerless – the rudder's damaged, but we've got to be stopped to fix it."

"That tells me nothing Jamie! Will it get us to the riverbank?"

Before Jamie could answer, the captain burst into the pilothouse. "I have the crew ready on the starboard side, Peerless."

Peerless didn't take his eyes off the river current. "That's all we can do with this rudder and half a paddle wheel. We can't get the bow against the current when we tie up either, Captain. I'm taking her right at the bank."

"That's what I figured. Now I've got to tell Trey that he's the new first mate. We just lost Gunny."

"He fell off the boat?"

"Yes, trying to save a goddamned horse. Get us to the bank, Peerless. We need to see if he's still alive. Jamie, you stay here. I'm going back down."

Peerless spoke into the tube again. "Smitty – the old man was just up here." This is going to be tricky. We are still too fast and we can't turn her. We'll go against the bank and back the rudder as best we can to slow her down."

"Nothing else we can do?"

"Nope – I barely have rudder as it is. Just stay with me Smitty. It's going to be quick after the bell."

Trey Barton, the second mate, was one of the crew waiting to jump off on the starboard side and tie the boat. Five other young men were with him. Michael, Titus and Rafael were the ones with experience. The other two were on a steamboat for the first time.

Captain Bridges walked to Trey. "You are the first mate now. You will stay on the boat no matter what happens – understand?"

Trey's face was expressionless. He knew things were starting to fall apart. The fact that Gunny had fallen into the water with a horse had already made its way around the boat.

Trey looked at the fast approaching river bank and started to speak, but Captain Bridges spoke first. "This landing isn't going to be easy, but we don't have a choice. You know what needs to be done."

"Aye sir." At that moment, they heard the paddle wheel spin hard again – then the stern slid around to the river bank.

"Great Smitty! Keep it up." All five crewmen were perched on the edge of the deck with ropes already tied to the cavels. Michael, Titus and Rafael were given the job of securing the stern.

"Be ready men!" shouted Trey. CLANG sounded the stopping bell. "Now men now!"

The men jumped into the water. They could not feel any ground beneath them. Titus swam to the bank as fast as he could while Rafael and Michael struggled with the heavy rope in the water.

CLANG sounded the backing bell. Smitty yelled, "I got it Peerless, here we go!" Smitty opened the throttle for the paddle wheel to spin backwards toward the river bank.

"Come on men!" yelled Trey.

Captain Bridges came up behind Trey and shouted, "Get to the bank, men!"

Rafael and Michael swam harder and reached the riverbank. Titus grabbed the rope from them and ran with it to a tree he spotted. He reached the tree and pulled the rope around it. Rafael and Michael raced to help him. The paddlewheel started backing the boat, then it clattered and stopped.

"Damn it, Peerless! We've lost it! The paddle wheel is gone," said Smitty into the tube. The current was not as strong at the riverbank as it was on the main stream, but it was still too much to secure a 113-ton boat while it was still moving.

Captain Bridges yelled, "Hold it!"

Michael, Rafael and Titus grabbed the rope and tried to brace it against a tree trunk, but it kept slipping through their hands.

Captain Bridges saw the rope moving too fast and yelled, "Let go! Let go! His order, however, came too late. The rope skinned two of Michael's fingers. He yanked his hand away and cried out in pain. Then they all let go. The rope slid around the tree and down the riverbank into the water. The boat drifted away in the current with both ropes still attached to the cavels. The other two crewmen were not able to get their rope even close to a tree.

Captain Bridges shouted to the men on the river bank. "Get down the bank as fast as you can! We'll try again down river!"

That was the last thing they heard as the stern of the boat followed the current away from the riverbank.

"Smitty can you give me anything forward!"

Smitty yelled, "More buckets broke off and jammed the wheel when she backed up. I've got nothing!"

Captain Bridges yelled as loud as he could, "Get an axe to to the wheel!" Will heard the captain and watched Trey grab an axe close to one of the wood piles. He ran with it to toward the paddle wheel, but tripped and hit his head on a post supporting the upper deck. Trey dropped the axe and fell to the deck. Will saw what the captain wanted, so he grabbed the axe off the deck and ran to the stern. There he saw a broken piece of wood jamming the paddle wheel on the larboard side. He raised the axe above his head and brought it down hard.

The captain saw Trey slowly sit up and touch his head. "Trey, what happened?"

Trey saw blood all over his hand. "I don't know."

"Stay here. Don't move. I'll get help."

Captain Bridges continued around the main deck trying to calm everyone aboard, but he feared the worst. He just left five men behind in a botched landing. On top of that, he had already lost his first mate, and now his second mate looked to be badly injured. The river current continued pushing the stern away from the bank. The boat was spinning out of control.

Martin Clearman knew how serious things had become. He ran up and down the main deck yelling, "Get to the middle of the boat now!" Miles, Ian and Nate did everything they could to calm the horses.

Gretchen pointed to the river bank. "The front is going to hit the rocks! The captain saw it too. He knew they were too close. He thought *we're dead in the water.*"

Peerless knew they would hit. He just didn't know how bad it would be. He desperately tried to use the boat's rudder against the current to somehow deflect the boat off the rocks or lessen the blow. He knew a straight-on collision with the rocks would sink the boat. He had to make the right decision, but was running out of options.

"Peerless!"

"What Smitty?"

"The wheel's turning!"

Peerless' eyes widened. He immediately reached for a cord above him. *CLANG* rang the backing bell.

"Peerless, you want to try–"

"Now, Smitty now! back-er-up! We're going to hit." The paddle wheel began to turn. "More, Smitty! More!"

"That's all we have, Peerless!" The boat slowed, but it

still continued toward the rocks.

The captain thought, *I'll be damned – we have the wheel again!* Then he yelled, "Everyone back! We're going to hit! Brace yourselves!" The bow continued toward the rocks while the stern followed the current away from the river bank again. When the impact occurred, the entire boat shuddered. The horses neighed and pulled against their ties. The howls of Samson could be heard throughout the boat. Crew members and passengers not holding onto something were knocked off their feet.

Smitty felt the impact all the way back in the engine room and fell to the floor. He pulled himself back up and reached for the speaking tube. "How bad is it, Peerless?"

Peerless knew the impact was not fatal because he still had time to land the boat. "We're probably going to be taking in water, Smitty. We were able to glance off the rocks at the end. It could have been worse."

"Just tell me when you need it!"

"The stern is still coming around. The bow will point up river and then start to spin down river with the current. But before it does, it'll point at the south river bank – when that happens I'm going to need what's left of that wheel to spin hard for as long as it can. We're getting this boat back to that north bank, Smitty!"

Passengers were afraid. Their first thought was to jump off the boat and swim to the riverbank. Some made their way to the edge of the main deck to do just that. Captain Bridges saw Will coming back from the stern with the axe in his hand, then he looked at the passengers and yelled, "Everyone get to the middle of the boat and stay there!"

The bow of the boat slowly swung toward the south bank. "Now Smitty!" Drew Smithwood applied another burst of steam and the paddle wheel began to spin fast again.

"That's it, Peerless. We haven't got any more."

"All right – we're just a little faster than the river now. After we get past this set of rocks we'll go off the main stream again."

Smitty hadn't eaten in a long time. He had also been on duty way before the boat hit the log. He knew he had to keep going, but the heat was getting to him. He spoke into the tube, "How much longer?"

"Just a little more Smitty – stay with me – back her off a bit." Peerless' sole purpose now was to not over steer the boat and waste what little maneuverability it had left. They were past the rocks now. The boat made its way closer to a part of the river bank where a hill and a trail could be seen just past the trees. "Okay Smitty! More! Now! Hit it!" Peerless turned the rudder hard. The wheel pushed the stern almost parallel with the river bank. "Okay Smitty let off." The wheel almost stopped spinning.

Captain Bridges yelled to the remaining crew with ropes, "Get ready men!"

"Okay Smitty – the bank's too steep and we're still too fast. I've got to try and run her up."

Captain Bridges saw that Peerless was going to run the bottom of the hull up onto the river bank. He screamed at the passengers, "Stay on board and hang on! Suddenly everyone aboard felt a raking sound from the bottom of the boat. Then everyone felt the hull reverberate against the ground beneath it for several seconds. The boat's starboard side slid for seventy feet, then slid off the bank and re-entered the water. "Go men go!" yelled Captain Bridges to the crewmen who jumped from the stern with a rope. They ran with it as fast as they could to the trees, but were too late. The boat drifted away, and they were out of rope. Captain Bridges thought *not again.* The crew members at the bow desperately climbed over rocks to get to the trees. Captain Bridges shouted, "Come on men! It's all up to you!" One of the men reached a tree with the rope and got it around the trunk while another grabbed the end of the rope and began to pull it. Captain Bridges ordered additional crewmen to help at the bow. The current continued to push the untied stern away from the riverbank. The men at the bow hurriedly wrapped the rope around the tree another time and held on as best they could. Captain Bridges yelled, "Brace yourselves! The stern's going to hit!" The stern swung around like a pendulum in the current, and the larboard side crashed into the riverbank. Those passengers and crewmen that were not hanging onto something fell towards the larboard side of the boat. The bow was now pointing up river. Captain Bridges shouted, "Secure the stern against the bank!"

The *Cypress Queen* had finally come to a stop. Peerless let go of the wheel and sat on the floor, completely exhausted. Jamie placed his hand on Peerless shoulder, "My God – you did it!" That was the best stretch of piloting anyone on this river has ever seen! Peerless looked up and smiled. Jamie helped him up. "Come on – let's get out of here. It's over." Peerless walked out of the pilothouse to the rail and saw the trees and the steep rise of the land. Then he held onto the railing and looked down over the two larboard side decks.

Martin Clearman saw Peerless and yelled, "There he is!" Those gathered on the larboard side of the boat knew he was the one that had saved them, so they cheered. Captain Bridges quickly made his way up to the railing and placed his arm around his pilot's neck. Then quietly said, "Well done Peerless."

CHAPTER EIGHT
THE WOODS

"How much farther, Titus?" asked Michael.

"Not much. We should be there in about fifteen minutes the way the boat was moving."

Michael, Rafael, Titus and the other two crewmen had been walking for half a mile through rocky terrain mixed with trees on the north side of the Ohio River. They were doing their best to follow Captain Bridges' orders and get back to the *Cypress Queen* after the first attempted landing.

Rafael said, "What if they are not there?"

A frustrated Titus looked back at his crewman and said, "Look, Rafa. They will be there. I know the place the captain is going. I've been up and down this river many times with him. Trust me. They will land that boat."

Rafael continued walking in silence for a few more yards and raised his voice, "I hope you are right about this, Titus. They had no rudder and no paddlewheel. They could have been pushed to the south side of the river."

Titus shook his head. "I told you what I thought, Rafa – relax."

Michael looked both ways after hearing something and said, "What was that?"

Then, Titus heard the rustling of leaves behind them together with several *clicks*. He turned in the direction of the sounds and saw several bearded men with rifles.

They were some of the most wretched human beings he had ever seen. He couldn't believe that he hadn't smelled them sooner.

"Hands up, boys" said one of bearded men.

All five crew members from the *Cypress Queen* raised their hands.

The person who appeared to be the leader was tall and skinny with dark hair and an unkempt beard. He wore an old stained tan shirt and gray pants that were frayed at the bottom. "Yep, they're from the boat. Look at those uniforms! Boys, you're going to walk in front of us and do exactly as I say, or I will shoot you in the back – understand?"

Another gang member said, "You tell him, Dale."

Titus said, "Yes sir, we'll do just what you say."

"That's what I want to hear – now walk!"

Titus took the lead and walked in front of the other four crewmen down a trail northwest away from the river. After a quarter mile, Titus and the others reached a clearing where they could see a very disheveled man with a rifle standing over a slender muscular young man kneeling on the ground. They also saw another man with faded clothes having a great deal of difficulty controlling a horse with only one cross tie attached to the halter. As Titus walked closer, he could see the man on the ground was Gunny and Mirage was the horse trying to get away.

Meanwhile, after the *Cypress Queen* was secure, Captain Bridges pointed at the remaining crewmen on the boat and yelled, "Get the rifles and take places on the riverbank!"

A few minutes later, Will saw the crewmen positioning one of the gangplanks at the bow. Once the gangplank was lowered, they ran off the boat and pointed rifles to the trees.

Will saw Captain Bridges walking toward the bow and asked, "Captain, why the need for guns? I thought the gangs around here were gone?"

"The worst people were caught or killed, but there's always something going on because of all the river traffic – wait a second…"

The captain turned his attention away from Will, pointed and shouted at one of the crewman with a rifle. "You – get over there! No, by those trees!" He turned back to Will and said "We also need this perimeter of rifles because we've got to unload the boat to repair the hull. Otherwise, everyone stays on board."

"The hit on the rocks we took back there?"

"Yep. We need to see if we're taking on any water."

"So the horses need to come off?"

"That's right. We've got to unload as much cargo as we can, so the boat sits higher in the water. We'll be fixing the paddlewheel and the rudders at the same time. I hate to ask more of you and your friends, Will, but we've lost seven people including the first and second mates and we only have five more over there protecting us."

"What about the others we left back there? We know they're alive."

"We have to do *this* first. The remaining passengers and crew are my concern right now." Then Captain Bridges walked away saying, "Things are going to be happening pretty fast until we get this boat ready to go."

Will went back to the main deck where he saw Nate and his family together with Ian and Miles.

Miles was shoveling manure and asked, "What's happening now?"

Will took off his hat, scratched his head and said, "We've got to get all the horses off the boat. The remaining crew's going to be unloading most of the cargo so they can get a better look at the hull."

Miles glanced at the river bank. "What about Gunny and the rest of those men? Somebody needs to go out and find them."

"The captain says he's low on crew and's not searching until the boat gets fixed."

"That's a bunch of crap! We know they're out there. What if one of them is injured?"

"Yeah, I think he's overreacting. If he's not going to help them, then someone has to, right?"

Ian raised his eyebrows and reached for his rifle.

Nate looked at Abigail, who quickly snapped back, "Nathaniel, you're going to get yourself killed!"

Nate placed his hand on her shoulder. "Don't worry. It's going to be fine, honey. No one has shot anyone yet. They're probably only a couple of hundred yards away."

"Honey, yourself! You have a young child, and it's not fine! Why do you think those men have guns pointed at the trees?"

"Abby, there's no danger right now, but even if there was, I'm going to do what's right and you know it."

Tears formed in Abigail's eyes. "Haven't you changed our lives enough already without dying on us too?" Then she turned away from Nate – took Caleb's hand and walked away.

Will said, "I'm sorry Nate. You don't have to do this."

"You heard me, Will. The right thing to do is help those men."

After they armed themselves and saddled their horses, Will said. "Miles, if there is trouble out there, we only get one shot with these guns on a horse. You best go and get our father's swords too."

Northwest of the boat at the clearing on the trail, Dale said, "Get over there by that tree and sit down." Gunny's hands were tied in front of him and his shirt appeared to be have been cut diagonally down his back.

Titus reached out his hand, "You made it Gunny! We thought you were–"

Then, Titus felt a stinging hard slap to his back that knocked him face forward to the ground. He cried out in pain and felt blood coming from his back, then someone behind him said, "No talking, boy!"

Titus turned his head and saw the person who had been pointing a gun at Gunny now had a whip in his hand.

"Stay down right there, and don't move till' I say!"

"You heard what Jerrod said. Sit down, shut up and look at the ground," said Dale, then he motioned to the rest of the crew members to sit down in a circle facing Gunny.

The rest the crew slowly complied. Titus' eyes briefly caught Gunny's. He could see Gunny had been through a lot. He was almost shaking, but it was not fear that Titus saw. It was rage. He had never seen Gunny so mad. The rest of the gang members had rifles and stood behind the crew. After Dale was satisfied that he had control, he slowly walked behind Jerrod and said, "Did he tell you anything?"

Jerrod Graves, an ex-convict who had spent several years in the Indiana state prison system, stoically replied "Not a thing."

"We'll see about that now that *I'm* asking the questions." Dale looked at Gunny, then turned back to Jerrod and quietly said, "His pants look a little nicer than the others, but that's just an undershirt he's wearing."

"That's how I found the pretty boy, Dale. If he had a coat, he could've gotten rid of it. I don't know if he's an officer or not."

Dale whispered, "That boat will pay to get an officer

back, so let's try and find out. Give me the rifle – use the whip when I tell you." Dale walked toward the crew. "Now boys, I'm going to ask you a couple of questions, and you are going to answer me, or I'll let Jerrod here go to work on your backs with that whip again." Then Dale walked around them in a pompous manner. "Who here is the officer?" Not one of the crew moved or said a word, so Dale pointed at Titus and said, "Fine, we'll start with you." Then other gang members grabbed Titus by both arms and flattened him face first onto the ground.

Gunny shouted, "I'm the officer!"

Titus tried to pull away from the men holding him and yelled, "No he's not! I'm the officer. He's lying!"

Dale said slowly, "Someone's going to tell me the truth if I have to get Jerrod, here, to whip you all."

Michael yelled, "They're both lying! I'm the officer."

Dale looked at Jerrod and shrugged. "Very funny boat boy." Then he pointed to Gunny and Michael. "Okay boys – have it your way."

Four more gang members grabbed Gunny and Michael and forced their faces to the ground. Jerrod swung the whip over his head once and snapped it on Titus' back again. Titus winced, but he did not cry out.

Jerrod walked to Gunny, raised the whip and brought it down hard on Gunny's back. The blow produced an instant streak of blood. Gunny screamed in pain and struggled to get free, but the gang members holding him smashed his face into the ground.

Dale looked at Titus and Gunny and walked slowly toward Michael. "Maybe whipping's not the thing with you guys? Looks like you need a little more." After a few more steps, Dale placed his hand on the back of Michael's shirt collar and shook it. Michael's head jerked back and forth against the ground before Dale said, "I'm just going to kill you!"

Shamus and Ray Little were in their late forties, but looked much older. They represented a small piece of the criminal machinations that had plagued this part of the Ohio River for years. The decades of crime that had taken place along the river included theft, kidnapping and murder. The hideouts ranged from caves to boats and houses. As they rode up on their horses, they saw that Jerrod had whipped Gunny, and Dale was pointing his rifle at Michael's head.

Ray turned to his brother. "He can't get any more stupid can he?"

Shamus shook his head. "I know it. He's not getting any better."

"Look at the other one with the whip? What was his name again?"

"Jerrod I think."

Ray sat back in his saddle. "They don't come any crazier than that, do they?"

"Alright, Ray, I'll deal with it. I was wondering who we were going to send out to that riverboat captain. Now I know." Then Shamus placed his right index finger and thumb in his mouth. A loud shrill whistle followed, and the rest of the Little Gang turned and looked at their leaders like a pack of dogs hearing a command. Shamus dismounted, gave his horse's reins to Ray and walked calmly to Dale who had a surprised look on his face. Shamus took the rifle from Dale, gently placed it on the ground, and slapped Dale in the face so hard that he fell down. Shamus knew he had everyone's attention. He looked down at Dale – picked up the rifle – held the butt near Dale's face and said, "Are all the thoughts you come up with this stupid?"

The left side of Dale's face was striped with the red

marks of Shamus' four fingers. He stayed on the ground touching his face. "Shamus – what'd you do that for?"

Shamus shouted for the rest of the gang to hear. "These people you have here HAVE NO MONEY! We need them to actually *be alive* to *get* the money!"

Dale held a hand over his left cheek. "I was trying to find out who the officer was."

Shamus pointed at Gunny. "It's probably him, but it doesn't matter! Whoever he is, they'll know we have him because *you're* going to be the one to tell them!"

"Me? What if they–?"

"You're going to be the one to tell them how much money we want, or I'll kill you myself!"

Then Shamus walked to Ray, handed him Dale's rifle and hopped back on his horse. After he saw that he had everyone's attention again, he pointed his pistol at Dale and said, "Walk in front of me back to the steamboat."

Ray motioned to the others. "The rest of you men do the same. Gather the horses and that crew, and walk them in front of me to the house."

The crew proceeded on a wide dirt trail formed from generations of people that continuously used it as their access to the Ohio River. The line of gang members, horses and the boat crew measured almost forty yards. The procession of the gang and crew also found themselves squinting and shielding their eyes from the sun.

The other passengers on the *Cypress Queen* followed Will's lead and began removing horses from the boat. Clyde McConnell, from the boiler deck, saw Will and several others had even saddled their horses, and shouted, "What are you guys doing?"

"Clyde, you're a good man with a family. Don't worry about what we're doing."

"What about Nate over there, Will? He's a good man with a family too."

"Clyde, keep your voice down. Help unload the boat. I'll explain later."

On the trail heading northwest, Michael, with his head facing forward whispered, "Titus, how's your back?"

Titus did not want Ray or anyone else in the gang to see him talking, so he kept his face forward and said, "Hurts like hell."

Ray at the back of the line said to Jerrod, "I think those two in front are talking. Tell them to shut the hell up."

Jerrod yelled, "No talking up there!"

Titus looked down and whispered, "I'm not taking any more of this."

"You're going to get yourself shot."

"I don't care, Michael. Someone has to do something because Captain is going to protect that boat and the passengers first. He doesn't know it's only a few idiots that got the jump on us."

Ray saw they were almost to the house. Mirage, however, didn't like the new surroundings or the person walking him because of the constant jerking on his halter, so he stopped and pulled back. The gang member assigned to Mirage pulled on the lead rope hard and Mirage reared up on his hind legs.

Another one of the gang ran over and said, "Give me that horse!"

Then each man pulled on Mirage, so he lurched back to the right – pulled both gang members off their feet and dragged them twenty yards before they let go of the tie hanging from the halter.

Titus saw his chance and ran away south of the trail.

One of the gang members in the back yelled, "Stop!" and fired his rifle at Titus, but the ball missed and hit a tree. Ray drew his pistol and ran his horse at the rest of the crewmembers to prevent anyone else from running. He levelled his pistol at Michael and shouted, "Next one that runs dies right here!" Ray shouted at the two closest gang members on horseback, "Dewey! You and Lumas! Get that guy and bring him back if you have to drag him behind your horse! Jerrod, you stay with me."

Dewey said, "Yes sir!" and the two rode off into the woods after Titus while Ray and the rest of the gang marched the remaining crew up the trail to the house.

Titus James grew up in Cincinnati. His parents were slaves that came to Ohio by way of the Underground Railroad. He always loved the Ohio River and was able to find work on steamboats with Captain Bridges years ago. Dewey and Lumas didn't realize that he was running toward a part of the river bank he knew very well. Titus had seen the north bank of the Ohio River for years in the first legs of his travels to St. Louis and New Orleans. Now he heard horses behind him but did not care. He would lead them south through areas where horses could not follow.

Dewey thought he saw Titus as he was trying to maneuver his horse through the thick brush and said, "Lumas – Isn't that him?"

"I don't see a thing."

"You're no help. We're going too slow with these horses anyway. They can't get through this."

"Okay, let's tie em' up to those trees."

Dewey turned his horse to the east. "No, dumbass – he has to be going to the boat. Let's head him off this way."

Titus kept running as best he could through the mixed foliage and open areas. With each open area he saw, he waited momentarily to see or hear any movements. This exercise took time, but he finally made his way to an area that was less than half a mile from the boat.

Dewey and Lumas rode as fast as they could to try and cut Titus off. They could see the woods clearing ahead and the Ohio River beyond that.

Titus heard sounds behind him and saw a path next to long wide clump of trees. He ran into the trees and hid under vines that that ran throughout the underbrush – then heard voices now and remained perfectly still.

"You think we missed him?"

"There's no way he beat us here," Dewey said, "Walk your horse on this side of these trees, and I'll go around by the river."

Both men walked their horses slowly on either side of the trees. Lumas said, "He may be close, but that boat's not that far away now. What if they come looking for him this way?" Then, as they passed on either side of Titus, Lumas' horse tried to rear up.

Dewey immediately stopped his horse and carefully looked through the trees.

Titus knew he was in trouble. If he did nothing, he would eventually be caught, but if he moved he would be killed.

CHAPTER NINE
THE SWORD

Titus decided that he would not be taken without a fight. He quietly reached for a rock with his right hand and slowly rose up behind a tree. Lumas was still having problems controlling his horse and had unknowingly passed him. Dewey did his best to see through the trees on the other side. Then Titus jumped out from behind a tree and threw a rock, which hit he left hind quarter of Lumas' horse. The horse reared and Lumas dropped his rifle in a frantic attempt to hold the reins.

Dewey saw what happened through the trees – then he saw Lumas' rifle hit the ground. He knew Titus was close but still couldn't see him. Dewey decided that he had to get the rifle first and rode his horse as quickly as he could through the trees. Titus saw Dewey exit the trees right in front of him and jumped high in the air with both arms extended. Dewey felt the impact of Titus fists under his right armpit. Titus fell on the ground behind the horse and rolled, but as Dewey was falling, his left heel slipped through the stirrup. When Titus looked up, he saw a terrified look on Dewey's face. Then Dewey screamed, as his frightened horse violently dragged him away. Titus saw him desperately trying to get free, but Dewey was never able to reach the stirrup. After being dragged twenty yards, the back of his head hit the ground. After ten more yards, his forehead hit the base of a tree because the horse was trying to knock loose what-ever he was dragging.

Titus picked up Dewey's rifle. He saw that Lumas regained control and was now galloping his horse back, so he cocked the rifle, then aimed and waited for the horse to get closer. He didn't have a clear shot at Lumas, so he lowered the rifle and ran straight at the horse waiving it back and forth. The horse saw the object and turned to the right, then Titus raised the rifle and fired. The ball hit Lumas on the left shoulder. He fell off his saddle backwards and hit the ground. Titus walked calmly toward the gang member, and when Lumas tried to stand, Titus hit him in the forehead with the rifle butt. Lumas fell back to the ground unconscious while his horse kept running to the west.

On the main trail southeast back to the steamboat, Shamus said, "All right Dale – this is it – stop right where you are." Shamus dismounted, tied his horse to a tree and said, "This is where you walk to the steamboat – tell them you must speak with the captain and say just what I told you to say."

"But what if they–"

Shamus pointed his pistol at Dale. "You heard me."

On the *Cypress Queen*, almost all the horses had been walked to the bow and unloaded from the larboard side gangplank. Clyde McConnell saddled one of his other horses and walked to Will and Miles.

Gretchen saw him walking towards Will, Miles, Nate and Ian and shouted from the boiler deck, "What are you doing?"

"These men need help Gretchen!"

"Gretchen saw the other men had weapons and shout-ed back, "Clyde, you're in no condition to do whatever you think it is you're doing!" Besides, it's been years since you've shot a gun. You need to think about me and Sammy!"

Captain Bridges had been at the back of the hurricane deck supervising the paddle wheel and rudder repairs and saw the men on saddled horses. He also saw Gretchen shouting at Clyde. Several of the other passengers on the boiler deck, including Abigail, Caleb and Sarah, came to the railing to see what was happening.

The captain yelled, "It's all right, Gretchen. No one is going anywhere today except back on this boat after it's fixed."

Will yelled, "What about those men out there, Captain?"

"Will, I am the captain of this boat. I decide what happens – not you."

"I know, you're the captain – on the water."

"Will, we don't know what's out there yet. You *go,* and you might not come back."

"Tell you what, Captain, you handle the boat, and we'll bring back those men."

"You're not going anywhere Will."

"I'm paying for this trip, Captain."

"Men!" yelled the captain. Two of the crew that had their rifles pointed toward the woods turned around and pointed them at Will, Miles, Ian and Nate.

Then, one of the crew with a rifle still pointed to the woods yelled, "Captain – here comes someone!"

Captain Bridges saw a scraggly man with an unkempt beard walking toward the boat and shouted, "Who are you and what do you want?"

"My name is Dale Darnell. We have your men and want $300 for them. If I don't get the money by sundown and get to walk out of here with it, we will kill one of your men every hour until we get the money."

Will smirked, then leaned over to Miles and whisper-ed, "Not to sound callous, but even for a ransom they're *not getting,* that price sounds way too low. These guys can't be that smart."

Miles whispered back, "Maybe he forgot what he was supposed to say."

Then everyone heard a familiar voice from the rocks high above them yell, "He's lying!" Those that were looking at Dale turned their heads up to see Titus.

Dale immediately recognized Titus' deep voice and started to turn and run back toward the path, but he saw a rifle pointed at him now from another crewman. Then two other crew members walked to Dale and grabbed his arms.

Titus made his way down the rocks to Dale and said, "Did you miss me? Well here I am – alive and well with the truth about you idiots."

Captain Bridges, still looking down from the hurricane deck, shouted, "Titus! Who is this man and what has happened to your back?"

Titus, yelled back. "This is the little ass of a man that had me whipped, Captain. He had his men hold me with my face to the ground while one of them whipped me and Gunny like dogs!"

Captain Bridges shouted, "Gunny's alive?"

"Yes, and after the whipping, Dale, here, was going to shoot Michael in the head, but his boss pulled him aside, beat him down, and sent him out here with no gun. I bet the *hillbilly* is probably up the trail right now hiding behind a tree."

Dale kept trying to avoid Titus' eyes as he spoke.

"Dale, we aren't going to hold you down like your boys did me, because we aren't like you. Let him go!"

The two crew members unhanded him. Titus quickly faked a right fist to Dale's' face. Dale's hands went up to block the punch that never came. Instead, Titus punched him hard in stomach with his left fist. Dale went down to one knee, coughing and spitting, then placed a hand on the ground and spit again. It looked like he was finished, but his other hand reached toward the waist band of his pants. Titus briefly glanced at the horses that were saddled, but out of the corner of his left eye saw movement. Suddenly Dale sprang from the ground and swung his right arm backwards across his body. In his hand was a small knife. Titus quickly fell backwards and dodged the blade. Dale re-gripped the knife to stab Titus on the ground.

CRACK was the sound that came from a nearby rifle followed by a puff of smoke rising above Ian's face. *THIT* was the sickening next sound as the ball from Ian's rifle struck Dales' skull. Dale's dead body fell over Titus, and his knife landed on the ground. "We're wasting time!" yelled Ian. "Let's get those men back!"

Caleb, looking through the railing on the boiler deck, said to his mother "They whipped him bad, mommy. Look at his back."

"Abigail yelled down to Nate. "Nathaniel, did you hear what Titus said? Save those men – you hear!"

Nate grinned and shouted back up to the boiler deck. "We'll bring them back, Abby!"

"Kill as many of those bastards you can while you're at it!"

"Damn Nate!" Will said. "I love it. Let's get *her* a horse and a gun."

Nate calmly replied, "Will, this is serious. There will be hell to pay."

Titus pushed Dale's body off of him and shouted, "Give

me a horse now!"

Captain Bridges was still high above them all on the hurricane deck and shouted, "Titus, I can't let you go. That gang could be much larger than just the people you saw."

"Captain, I'm going to get Gunny and the others. They're still alive." Then he walked to Will and said, "Give me a horse."

Will turned to his friend and said, "Sorry Clyde. We need him more than we need you right now. He knows where to go. Give him your horse."

Clyde said, "The horse is yours, Titus – go!"

Captain Bridges threw his hands down and yelled at the crew members with rifles "It's alright men. Let them go!"

Titus took the lead with Will right behind him followed by Miles, Nate and Ian. As they rode away Miles said, "Ian, that was a little harsh with poor Dale don't you think?"

Ian kicked Dutch into a run and laughed. "That's what he gets for bringing a knife to a fist fight!"

Captain Bridges quietly said "God's speed, Will Richards."

Shamus heard a gunshot from somewhere around the boat and didn't figure things were going well with Dale, so he headed back up the road and hopped on his horse as quickly as he could. Shortly after that, he heard the sound of several horses running behind him.

Titus rode like a man possessed. He rounded one wooded curve on the trail after another. Will was right behind him and pulled back on his reins at times because Lucky never wanted to be behind another horse.

Titus rounded one more area and saw a horse and rider. "That's one of them Will – looks like Shamus. I got him!" Titus tried to get Clyde's horse to go faster. Then Shamus turned and fired his pistol at him. The ball was off target and missed, but the shot startled Titus's horse. Titus tried to regain control, but the horse started to slow down and buck.

Will shouted, "Yah! Lucky!" and slapped the reins. Shamus had been looking behind him every couple of seconds because he was alone on the trail, and now he had no way of reloading his pistol. The next time he glanced back, he saw a large black stallion closing on him quickly. Shamus knew he would be caught, so he turned sharply between two trees. Lucky was going so fast that he slightly overshot the area where Shamus turned. Will pulled both reins back slightly and to the right, then he felt Lucky lunge forward in a burst of speed to catch Shamus' horse again. Shamus looked back, but only briefly, because the trees were coming fast and the spaces were tight. At their speed, the sun's rays flickered rapidly through trees, making it very hard to see the trail. Will now was barely touching the reins. Lucky thought this chase was a game and seemed to know what to do in a forest. He remembered Jacobus saying, *He loves the trees from his time with Hawkeye.* Will only had to keep both legs on Lucky so a stirrup wasn't caught on a tree. Shamus heard them getting closer and couldn't believe it. He knew he would come out of the trees soon, though, and be back on the main trail to the house.

Titus said, "I can't see them, Nate."

"I know, they went into the woods too fast."

Titus glanced to the right again. "I bet they'll wind up coming out close to wherever that house is."

Miles looked around and yelled, "Yep let's get up there then – Ian, where are you?"

Titus said, "Wait! Look up there!"

Shamus came out of the trees, pulled his right rein and kicked his horse. A second later, Will and Lucky bolted out from the same area chasing Shamus. Lucky was taking loud breaths and snorting as he turned. His eyes were opened wide and his mane stretched out behind his neck as he went to a full gallop. Shamus looked back again and realized this black horse was going to run him down. He began to whip his reins furiously on either side of his horses' neck but it didn't help. Lucky was almost to the hind quarters of Shamus' horse. Will held the reins in his left hand and reached for the handle of his father's sword with his right. After a few more strides, Will got beside Shamus – raised the sword above his head – then brought it down hard across Shamus' back.

CHAPTER TEN
KILLERS
IN THE DARK

Shamus cried out as he fell from his horse and hit the ground. Then his horse ran for home. Miles knew the horse had to be stopped and slapped Chipper's reins.

Will saw them flying past and said, "Stop that horse, Miles!" Then he patted Lucky on the neck and whispered, "Good boy" in his left ear. After that, he walked to where Shamus was lying face down on the ground with his right arm trying to reach his bloodied back.

Will said, "That had to hurt?"

"*Who* are you?"

"You must've *not* done very well in school – did you?"

A few seconds past before Titus and Nate arrived. Then, Titus jumped off Clyde's horse, walked to Shamus, and said, "Little worse than a whipping...huh, Shamus?"

Shamus couldn't believe what he was hearing. He looked back at Titus. "*You* – how did you..."

"I just did, and by the way, your boys that came after me are dead – just like you're going to be if I don't hear from you what I want to hear right now."

Titus bent Shamus' right leg behind him at the knee and forced his left foot down on top of the right so both feet were bent all the way backwards to Shamus' rear end. Then, while keeping pressure on the left foot, he spun around and sat on Shamus' back pulling the left foot toward himself. Shamus felt pain in thighs, feet and back all at once and screamed.

"How much further is that house?"

"It's just up the path."

Titus pulled Shamus' left foot even harder against his right, then began to twist Shamus' left ankle. "Wrong answer."

Shamus face was forced much harder into the ground. He screamed a muffled scream and uttered the words "half...mile"

"Good dog – now – how many men and how many guns?"

"The men come and go. I don't know."

Titus frowned and twisted Shamus' left ankle so hard that his left foot became partially dislocated. The pain was unbearable.

Shamus gasped and whispered, "Seven men or eight...I swear."

"How many guns, Shamus? I'll do the other foot too."

"Eight rifles – five pistols..."

"Where will they be keeping the crew?"

"I don't know..."

"Wrong answer." Then Titus let the left foot go and started twisting Shamus' right foot.

Shamus let out another garbled scream into the ground, "Downstairs back room of the house."

"Dogs?"

Shamus was starting to pass out from the loss of blood from his back and whispered "No dogs..."

"Okay Will, let's go!"

Will watched Shamus' feet fall back to the ground as he lost consciousness and said "Titus, remind me to never make you mad."

"These are evil people, Will – I've seen what they–"

"Hey folks! Look what I found on the trail." Miles walked up on Chipper holding Shamus' horse by the reins at the same time Ian approached them from the opposite direction on Dutch.

Will said, "I knew you'd do it, Miles! If that gang saw Shamus' horse walk up to that house alone, it would've blown everything. Ian, where the hell have you been? You missed all the fun."

"I saw you had things under control, so I had a wee in the woods."

"We're in a life and death chase with goddamned Shamus, and you peel off for a pee?"

"I wasn't catching you anyway on that leviathan of a horse you saddled me with!"

"He was the only horse that could support your fat ass, Ian!"

Titus interrupted, "Men, this can wait."

Will shook his head. "Sorry Titus, but he's so...never mind...since the sun just set, let's wait till it gets a little darker before we approach the house. We can tie the horses over there."

The men tied their horses to trees and waited half an hour before taking all the weapons and ammo they could carry. They walked slowly in a straight line by for a quarter of a mile before Will put his hand up and whispered, "I smell smoke. Let's fan out, Miles. You and Ian go the the left – Nate, you and Titus to the right. Keep your voices low."

They began walking as slow and steady as they could while being careful not to step on anything that would make a sound under their feet if they could help it. After fifteen minutes, the faint outline of a structure became visible through the trees. Light smoke rose from the chimney. The house was a dilapidated, off white, two-story structure with a covered porch that stood in a clearing. It had seen better days. The woods came a little closer to the east side of the house in the back. The front of the house faced west and had a lit outdoor fire pit where an assortment of chairs and benches had been placed. About thirty feet from the house, on its north side, nine horses were tied to ropes stretched between the trees. One of the horses was Mirage. Will motioned for the men to quietly gather.

"What are you thinking, Will?" asked Nate

Will looked at Miles and pointed. "Miles, when it's dark, you and Ian make your way around to the front of the house in the woods. Set up a position there with both your rifles, but Ian does all the shooting from that distance."

Miles frowned and said "Ian?"

"Yes, you need to always be loading a rifle for Ian and then move after the first couple of shots. We want them to think everything is coming from the front, and that you guys are more than two people. The rest of us will come in from the back once we see them occupied. Oh, and don't start shooting till dawn."

After the sky was completely dark, Ian and Miles began their painstaking journey eighty yards through the woods. They would have to move west then north, unnoticed, all the way to where they would face the fire pit and the front of house. They were very careful not to step on twigs or small branches that might snap. This quiet process took half an hour in the dark. Finally, they crept to a place west of the front of the house where they had a clear shot.

Inside the house, Ray said, "Give me that whisky. I'm going outside to wait for Shamus." "I'll have some of that too, Ray," said another gang member.

The only well-fed member of the gang was of French lineage and their cook. He was vigorously cleaning a chicken at the sink when Ray said, "Hey Bouler, do we have any of that meat from last night left?"

"No, but I'm preparing something new – even as we speak."

"We had leftovers when we went to bed last night."

"You men have been gone all day. I didn't know when you were coming back."

"You ate it all again, didn't you?"

"It was going to spoil."

"I should've known."

Bouler raised an index finger to the bottom of his chin and hurriedly said, "Ray, here – take this nut and berry plate to the fire with the whisky now, and I'll bring out the chicken to fry within minutes..."

"Just hurry it up, Bouler. Remember, you still have to watch over that boat crew in the back of the house."

Bouler crossed his arms and tried to stick out one of his chins. "They're tied up and on the floor, and I have the strap if anyone moves."

Ray looked at the floor and shook his head, as he walked out the front door with the nut and berry plate. Several of the gang saw the plate in his hand and said, "What the hell is that?"

Ray placed the plate on a log. "He ate the rest of the dinner from last night when we were gone."

"Again? Shit, Ray! What good is a cook that eats all of our food before we do?"

"Ray motioned with both hands to tamp down the complaint. "I know, I know. I'll talk to Shamus about it when he gets back, but right now – let's eat what we have."

As the evening progressed, the Little gang consumed all the fried chicken and many rounds of whisky.

Ian patiently watched and whispered to Miles, "Like shooting fish in a barrel."

"They're getting sauced, Ian." Then Miles gestured to a set of trees thirty feet away and whispered, "After you shoot from these trees, I'll be over there with another loaded rifle."

"Perfect – When I start shooting, you keep putting a loaded rifle in my hand, and we'll be back to the boat before we know it."

Will, Nate and Titus had already taken a position in the woods south of the house where they could see the front of the house and some of the back area.

Nate watched the party at the fire pit for a few more minutes and whispered to Will, "I bet one of them is going to get up and pee in the woods."

"That'll be one less right?"

Nate smiled and said, "I'll find a good hiding place."

"Be careful you don't spook their horses. We don't want any of those bastards reaching for a gun too soon."

"I'll be set in ten minutes."

Ian whispered, "Miles, Nate went behind the house."

"Do you think they're going to the back now?"

"No – Will and Titus stayed put."

A gang member near the fire sat up when he suddenly realized that he needed to relieve himself. After standing, he moved in too much of a hurry and hit his right foot on a log, but caught himself before he fell and hopped on his left leg several times to avoid hitting the ground. The episode covered ten yards before he was able to regain his balance. Then he made the mistake of looking back at the fire.

One of the gang yelled, "It's all right – nobody saw!" A

chorus of laughter peaked after ten seconds and slowly tapered off when their distressed gang member disappeared into the trees.

Ian whispered, "Nate's at the other side of the house now – and look – that poor dumb sot is going to have a wee in the woods over by him!"

"Looks like our four outside are getting ready to be three, Ian."

Nate had positioned himself against a tree that was between the horses and the house. When the inebriated gang member staggered past, Nate quickly placed his right hand over the man's mouth and slit his throat with a large knife. The man struggled briefly in Nate's arms before he died. Nate slowly let his body rest on the ground so as to not make any noise. Those still by the fire simply assumed their friend went into the house once he relieved himself.

Will found himself fighting sleep. All the men from the *Cypress Queen* had been awake almost twenty-four hours now. Ian nudged Miles when he saw Ray start to move.

The conversation around the fire had tapered off before Ray thought about his brother again and asked, "Hey has anyone seen Shamus yet?"

Another gang member stood and looked for Shamus's horse but didn't see it. "No, I don't see the horse, Ray. Do you think something's wrong?"

Those were his last words. *KERPACK* was a familiar sound for these gang members, but this time they didn't see from where the shot was fired. They just noticed their friend, who was talking to Ray, fly backwards because he had been shot in the head.

Miles whispered louder, "Ian, it's not dawn yet!"

"We were going to lose our fish! Now move."

Will couldn't believe it. "What in the hell? Titus, it's not even dawn yet. We've got to get back behind the house now."

As they ran, Will said, "*Ian, don't shoot until dawn*! How hard is that to follow? We should have left him in George Town!"

Titus and Will made their way back to the woods behind the house. They were breathing hard and waiting for Nate. Titus quietly said, "I guess we're fighting in the dark now."

Nate ran around from the north side of the house, then quickly got down beside Will and Titus. After he took a couple of deep breaths he said, "That crazy Scott is going to get us all killed."

The drunken gang members remaining by the fire crawled on the ground to find their guns by the firelight. Miles handed Ian another loaded rifle. One of the drunks, in an unexpected effort to reach the front door, jumped up and had almost taken three steps before Ray heard a *CRACK* followed by the sound of a ball hitting the back of the man's head. The man fell dead on the ground next to him. Ray didn't move for almost a minute, then slowly glanced west and thought he was too exposed. He didn't want to be the next to die, so he decided to use the dead body as a shield; and in one quick move, rolled over the body so it was between him and the woods. Then Ray yelled to those inside the house, "Jerrod, send Wyrick out and get me inside!"

Ian whispered, "Faster Miles! You're too slow!" Miles' realized his sole purpose in life right now was to load and reload the rifles for Ian.

Will quietly said, "Well, it sounds like Ian's still killing them. I'll give him that. Let's give him a few more seconds since he's on a roll."

Two rifle barrels suddenly broke through the windows on either side of the front door. Then both rifles fired haphazardly into the woods. A split second later, a young man shot through the front door and dove from the front porch toward the horses with a pistol in his hand. Before he hit the ground, he tucked his head and rolled – then jumped back to his feet and dove again.

Ian immediately saw him and said to Miles, "A runner!" He tracked the young man with his rifle like wild game on the move and fired. The ball missed Wyrick and hit a tree. While planning his next move, Wyrick noticed the man Nate killed a few feet away.

As soon as Ray heard Ian's shot, he pushed up from the body he was hiding behind and ran for the house. He was so afraid of being shot from behind, he tripped on the last step to the porch, and fell face first through the partially open doorway. Then Jerrod slammed the door behind him.

Ian sat back behind his tree. "Did you see the way that young man moved Miles?"

"Yes."

"Have you ever killed anyone, Miles?"

"No."

"Miles – Will pretends to have fun and joke around, but he is very serious *inside* about what he does. You need be that serious right now."

"I'm serious too, Ian."

"Miles, that young man is wiry and fast. He is probably the best they've got. I can't move like that."

"You want me to go after him, don't you?"

Ian looked to where Wyrick entered the trees and slowly said, "Right now you need to be thankful of the dark and *work within it* to kill him, because if you don't, he will most assuredly kill us." Ian saw Miles mentally trying to prepare himself to fight another person with weapons in the dark. Miles reaction to the situation was to go down to his knees and throw up. Ian watched this continue for a few seconds then said, "It's okay, but you must go now."

First, Miles made sure he had his knife and rifle then he looked intently for any movement in the woods. Seeing none, he got to his feet and ran as fast as he could to a large tree about thirty yards to his left. Fearing that he would be shot from somewhere in the dark at any second, he went down behind the tree too quickly and hit his left elbow on the trunk. Ian saw Miles' awkward move, shook his head, and thought, *God, help the goof live through the day.*

Donnie Wyrick was a southern Illinois athlete while in school. He came from a broken home and wound up hanging around the Ohio River with the wrong people. The young man had been with this gang for only two months. Wyrick knew these trees to the west of the house. He efficiently and quietly made his way to where he thought the shooter was hiding.

Will said, "All right guys, on Ian's next shot we go."

Inside the house, Ray and the remaining gang members were trying their best not to be die. Ray would not place himself anywhere near a window. Jerrod was cautiously trying to peer into the woods to catch a glimpse of who was killing them.

Ray, safely from across the room said, "Don't worry. Wyrick'll get 'em!"

"You bet he will Ray – I'm just having a look." In Jerrod's mind, there was still a chance to be a hero. Jerrod thought that if he assumed the smallest possible profile at the window, he would be able to see the shooter, so he positioned his rifle barrel to only protrude inches from the window while he crouched below its corner in the least vulnerable spot.

Ray said, "You see anything yet, Jerrod?"

Jerrod looked keenly down his rifle barrel and said, "I think I do."

Ian turned his attention back to the house. The light from the outside fire still illuminated the porch, so Ian aimed at the northernmost window where he believed the last shot was fired. He thought he saw the faint outline of a rifle barrel from that window but wasn't sure. He had no other target, so he decided to shoot right above whatever he saw. Ian's rifle made another loud *CRACK*. At the same time Jerrod saw a brief flash of light in the woods, and in less than a second, the ball from Ian's rifle hit Jerrod in the orbit of his left eye. Ray watched his body propel backwards. It finally came to rest when the back of Jerrod's head hit the kitchen floor like the end of a whip.

Ray, fearing another shot coming into the house, crawled quickly on his hands and knees to the staircase in order to be further away from the windows. He saw the gang was losing this fight and decided to hedge his bets, so he yelled, "Bouler, bring me the officer and make sure his hands are tied."

Ian remained motionless and carefully looked for something else to shoot, but there was nothing – no movement and no target. What was worse was the fact that he heard nothing around him. He had to do something. He thought Miles and the agile gang member were playing a deadly game of cat and mouse about forty yards away. The least he could do would be to give his position away and flush the speedy menace out of his hiding place so Miles might see him move first.

Behind the house, Will said, "All right, on Ian's next shot we go."

Ian selected the window just to the south of the front door this time, but intentionally fired below it because he could not see anyone from the house and didn't want to shoot his friends if they were entering it. *CRACK.* The gang members at the front of the house got down again when they heard another ball hit the house.

Will said, "That's it! Come on!"

Titus, Nate and Will ran toward the back door. Will was first to the door and hit it with his shoulder. When the door flew open, Will raised his pistol to fire. He saw the boat crew to his right tied up on the floor. A wall separated the front of the house from the back with a small hallway joining the two. A small lamp on a narrow table in the hallway cast some light toward the back. The smell in the house was horrible.

One of the remaining gang members at the front of the house heard noises coming from behind him, and without looking back said, "Bouler, check that out."

Bouler descended the stairs after helping Ray pull Gunny to the top. He had almost reached the bottom when he heard Ray shout, "When you get down those stairs check those crewmen again. I thought I heard a noise!"

He assumed the other crew members were trying to move around again and grabbed the leather strap he was using to occasionally beat them if they didn't stay down.

With the strap firmly grasped in his right hand, he said, "Okay, who wants some more of this?" and moved into the hallway. Will was already there pointing a pistol at him. Bouler froze. Will knew he had only one pistol shot in this fight. He also saw the gang member downstairs who had just ordered Bouler to check the back of the house. This man still had a rifle pointed out the front of the house. Will quickly dismissed Bouler as being any sort of a threat and, at the last second, raised his pistol slightly above Bouler's head and fired through the hallway. Bouler's involuntary reflex to the pistol discharging in front of him was to quickly flail the strap, let out an odd scream, and crouch on the floor. Will stepped back to avoid Bouler's strap from hitting him in the face. The gang member peeking through the window at the front of the house was now reaching for the middle of his back and writhing in pain on the floor. After Bouler collected himself, he lunged at Will, swinging the strap over his head. When the strap came down, Will extended his left arm, allowing the strap to hit it. He then turned his left hand over – grabbed the end of the strap and pulled Bouler to him. Bouler let go of the strap, but he had already been pulled off balance. Nate was next to Will on his left side as the rotund cook came between them. Nate had a loaded pistol in his left hand and a hatchet it the right. He swung the butt end of the hatchet and hit the unfortunate cook in the back of the head. Bouler fell to the floor unconscious.

Will and Nate then saw someone dart past the other end of the hallway, and Nate started to go after whoever it was.

Will said, "Wait!" and looked back at Titus, who had gone into the room on the right to free the crew members. He thought for a second and sat the unconscious Bouler upright. Will took off his own hat and quickly pulled it down over Bouler's head, then with his left hand grabbed Bouler by the collar, and with his right hand, grabbed the back of Bouler's belt. Will raised Bouler, and walked in front of Nate holding the cook's body upright like a shield. As soon as he reached the end of the hallway, Will held Bouler out a few inches into the front room toward the left. A rifle shot rang out and hit

Bouler in the head, knocking Will's hat to the floor. Nate went behind Will and Bouler's body to where the shot was fired and peeked past the hallway to the left. He saw another skinny gang member in the corner who had just fired the shot desperately trying to reload his rifle. Nate, not wanting to use his pistol shot yet, put the hatchet in his right hand and threw it end over end. The hatchet hit the skinny gang member in the chest. The gang member fell backwards against the wall and instinctively pulled the hatchet from his chest, but the effort only resulted in him losing more blood. Will dropped Bouler and picked up his hat, which had a gunshot hole in it. Nate grabbed his hatchet from the skinny man, who was quickly losing consciousness. Will and Nate saw no one else in the front room of the house alive. There were only dead bodies on the floor and blood was everywhere. Will looked back, but did not see Titus.

Back in the woods on the west side of the house, Wyrick patiently waited for the shooter to show himself. After the last shot he knew he would get to him before there was another. Wyrick ran to Ian's position weaving through the trees like a deer.

Miles was still crouched behind the large tree gripping his rifle. The wiry gang member's footsteps moved faster and faster then suddenly stopped. Wyrick saw a squirrel inexplicably dart from a nearby tree and almost run into him before it changed directions. Wyrick knew the squirrel wouldn't naturally come at him unless it was running from something else. He assumed someone was closer to him than the shooter and jumped behind a tree. When the footsteps stopped, Miles feared the worst. He thought this person in the dark somehow knew where he was now. Ian heard footsteps to the left of him. He also heard other shots and screams from within the house and figured Will, Nate and Titus were inside.

Wyrick couldn't stand it. His job was to get to the shooter, and he was failing. He thought he would throw something to distract whoever was close to him, so he picked up several pebbles and threw them with a flick of the wrist so they would scatter over several yards. Miles heard multiple sounds to the left of him hitting tree trunks and branches. He instinctively turned his head when he heard the sounds. At that moment, the young killer rushed to Ian's position. Miles heard the footsteps and ran out from behind the tree with his rifle pointed in front of him. Wyrick didn't see Miles at first because he was so focused on getting to the person doing the real damage to his gang. When Miles saw Wyrick, he pulled the trigger, but his rifle misfired.

CHAPTER ELEVEN
THE WILDCARD

Wyrick immediately heard the *click* of Miles' rifle without the small explosion of the percussion cap. He knew someone pulled a trigger to kill him, so he ran in the direction of the *click* before the gun could be reloaded. Miles, however, had already dropped his rifle and hid behind two trees with a knife. When Wyrick ran past the trees, he heard a sudden crunch of leaves, then saw a person in the air with a knife in his hand. Wyrick quickly jumped backwards, but stumbled and dropped his pistol to brace his fall. When he hit the ground, however, his arm was too straight and he jammed his left shoulder. Wyrick didn't care. He jumped to his feet in an instant, pulled his own knife, and swung it at Miles' face. Miles thought he had avoided the blade, but an instant later felt blood oozing from his right cheek. Miles saw that he couldn't get close without being cut first because the lanky young man had a much greater reach. He needed something, *anything,* to block the blade coming at him. He spotted a forked tree branch about five feet long on the ground and picked it up with his left hand before Wyrick swung the knife again. Miles blocked the knife with the branch and moved directly at Wyrick, who slashed at it with his knife. Then Miles pointed the branch at his face again. Wyrick slashed at the ends of the branch and tried to get around it, but he never tried to grab the branch with his left hand. Miles thought, *He can't move the other arm.* At that moment, Miles changed. His fear was gone, and he suddenly found himself acting like a wild animal trying to kill another animal. He kept running and jamming the branch in Wyrick's face no matter which way the young man moved. Wyrick kept backing up and fell to the ground again. When he hit the ground, he wasn't able to brace his fall with his left arm, so he hit the ground on his injured shoulder. Miles was on him like like a cat and slashed Wyrick's right thigh as hard as he could. Wyrick somehow jumped to his feet and swung the knife again, but his leg bled heavily. Miles, running completely on adrenaline, kept thinking, *I am not going to be the one to die!* Wyrick tried to use his height and superior reach with an overhand motion to knock the branch downwards, but the move exposed his right arm, and Miles slashed it as hard as he could. Wyrick lost strength in his right hand now, and had to grip the knife tighter or he would drop it. He desperately lunged at Miles with his right arm and fought through the branch this time, but Wyrick lost his footing and fell forward. Without being able to brace his fall with his left arm, he hit the ground face first. Miles dropped the branch and used his left hand to hold Wyrick down. The young man kept trying to get up, but Miles stabbed him repeatedly in the back until he was dead.

Miles shook. He was covered in sweat and still bleeding from his face. He sat on the ground, dropped his knife, and tried to come to terms with the fact that he just killed another human being. After a minute, the sun's early rays made everything more visible. He looked at Wyrick's body next to him along with yards of blood on the ground and cried. Then he glanced at the tree branch next to him and thought, *what have I become*? Less than a minute passed before his thoughts turned to the rest of his friends who were still fighting, so he picked up Wyrick's pistol and walked back to find his rifle.

Inside the house, Will went back to Titus who had freed the rest of the crew. Titus, however, had a very troubled look on his face.

Will said, "What's going on?"

"Gunny's not here."

"Where the hell is he then?"

A voice from upstairs yelled, "He's up here with a gun to his head, and if I see one foot on those stairs – he dies!"

Will looked back at Titus, threw his arms down by his side, and said, "Damn it!" Then he composed himself. "Everyone – but me – get out of the house! I'll talk to this guy. What's his name?"

Michael said "Ray, He's the brother of Shamus."

Will whispered back, "*Was* the brother of Shamus."

As the crew members went out the back door, Will tapped Nate on the arm and softly said, "While I talk to Ray up there, will you sneak through the woods and get to Ian and Miles?"

Nate rolled his eyes, "Sure, Will – what do you want me to tell them?"

Will motioned for Nate to follow him to the back of the house. They stepped past the back door and kept their voices low. "You're going to have to hurry. Tell Miles to come out of the woods when I yell at him, and for him to lay his rifle down so Ray can see him doing it."

"Okay Will, he's going to love that. What about Ian?"

"Tell him, to shoot any person that's not Gunny – or one of us – whenever he has the chance."

"Okay, but *I'm* not walking out from the woods with Ray up in the window."

Will rolled his eyes. "Nate, Miles is going to be fine, and if any of this gets to be longer than an hour, we'll do something else. Just tell Ian to stay put until this is over."

"So I'm out there with Ian as long as it takes, too?"

"Yes, but don't let Ray see you getting back there because the sun's up now. We have to be patient until we see how this starts to play out. I want to keep all our options open."

At that point, Will went back in the house and yelled upstairs, "Ray, my name is Will Richards. You win! We just want to get to St. Louis. I'll pay the $300 you want and you give us that man and no one else has to die."

Ray yelled, "You've already killed everyone but me. How can I trust you?"

"Ray, you're right. We got this far but no further – so you get to live and you get the money. We just want the mate back unharmed."

"How do I know you'll keep your word?"

"Ray, you're not getting the money and getting to harm the mate too. It's your choice – one way you die and the other way you don't."

"I think you'll kill me no matter what."

"There's no other deal for you, but I'll tell you what..." Will paused and shouted back up the stairs. "...I'll make it four hundred dollars! And if we see him walking down that road to us – you get to live, and we go back to the boat."

"The shooter in front of the house will kill me."

"Ray, I'm going to place my money belt with $400 in it on one of these chairs out by the fire pit. Then I'm calling my man with the rifle out of the woods, and we'll walk away with the others and wait to see Gunny on that road."

"You're bluffing, Richards."

"No – I'm walking out the front door now, but if you kill me, I promise you, these guys will kill you."

Will walked out the front door and down the steps to the fire pit, but had to step over one of the dead gang member's bodies to get to the chair. He held his money belt in the air and yelled for the benefit of Ian.

"Here it is Ray – all for you! Just let the kid go!" Then Will opened part of the money belt and showed Ray the cash.

Ray's curiosity took him to a few inches from the right side of the window frame where he saw the money in Will's hands and yelled back, "The shooter, Will!"

Will turned to the woods and shouted, "Miles, come out! Put your rifle down. It's over." Then he waited.

Neither Miles, nor any sound came from the woods.

Will glanced to the upstairs window and said, "Maybe he didn't hear me." Will yelled as loud as he could, "Miles! Come out! It's over!"

To Will's amazement, Miles actually walked out in the open with a bloodied face. He placed his rifle on the ground slowly – stood with his hands in the air, and walked straight to Will, who couldn't believe it. Will looked back at the house and said, "That's it, Ray! We're leaving, but we'll be back if that crewman doesn't come walking down that path pretty soon."

Miles kept walking slowly toward the south side of the house away from Ray's window. Will met him and they both walked behind the south side of the house together. After they were out of Ray's sight, Miles said, "You're a damned idiot, and I'm a bigger idiot for following you out here. I had to *actually* kill a young man out there today or he would have killed me!"

"The day's not finished yet, Miles. You might get another chance."

"Go to hell, Will."

They kept walking east out of sight of the house and

found Titus sitting on the ground with the other crew-men. Will leaned down – placed his hand on Titus' shoulder and asked, "Will you go back and position the crew to watch the house by the back door. We may need to go in again.

"This had better work, Will. Do you hear what I'm saying?"

"It's going to work – just a little bit longer okay? Ray's going to either take the money and run or he's going to get shot."

Then Will stood, tapped Miles on the back, and started to run down the path saying "Let's get the horses."

Titus and the other crew members began slowly walking back to the the trees behind the east side of the house. They were out of Ray's sight if he were to look through the upstairs windows in the back of the house. Ian and Nate remained hiding in the woods in front of the house to the west. Will and Miles ran like they have never run before to get Chipper and Lucky.

Ray watched all the others leave from a back window upstairs and walked back to his tied and gagged hostage. "Looks like your friends have left you *Gunny*, now that I know your name!" Then he slapped Gunny, and his head was knocked as far as the ropes holding him to the chair allowed. "This Richards character is playing me. He thinks he gets whatever he wants, but he's getting the wild card today."

Ray went downstairs and stepped over the dead bodies of his former gang and emptied all the lanterns' fuel onto the inside corners of the house. Then he looked at the horses through the front window's broken glass. He saw that one was still saddled with a bridle and smiled. After that, he walked to the back of the house and saw the back door frame was hanging off the wall with the door swinging slightly back and forth. He also saw Bouler's leather strap on the ground close to his body, so he folded the strap and wedged it under the door to keep it from blowing open. The wind was blowing from the south, so he started a fire at that end of the house.

CHAPTER TWELVE
RETRIBUTION

Flames and smoke came from within the south side of the house and spread rapidly to the outside. Ian quietly said, "He's burning it, Nate!"

"Do you see Ray?"

Ian looked at the porch, and then spent several seconds trying to see through the smoke that was starting to engulf the horses. He saw no human legs between any of the horses and said, "No – nothing."

As soon as Titus and the crew members approached the house again, they smelled smoke and hurried to the last line of trees before the house. Flames were consuming the south side of the house and blowing to the north.

Michael said, "What do we do? Is Ray still there?" Then the crew members heard the sound of horses. It was Lucky and Chipper running up behind them.

Will dismounted and gave his reins to Miles. "Anyone come out?"

Titus said, "No one yet."

"We've got to know about the front. Watch the back door while I check with Ian." Then Will ran to the south side of the house and yelled, "Ian, anyone come out yet?"

Ian's voice bellowed from the trees. "Not a soul." Then Ian and Nate quickly ran forward to a tree nearer the house, since their presence in the woods was no longer a secret.

Will yelled, "Keep watching!"

The flames were very hot. Dark smoke blew north away from Will. He looked at the area around the fire pit and saw his money belt was still on the chair. The wind continued to push the fire to the north side of the house where Gunny was being held.

From the shouts outside, Ray heard that Will's friends never left and thought, *Of course he lied*. The horses next to the north part of the house tried to pull from their ties because the black smoke stung their eyes and they could no longer breathe fresh air.

Nate kept watching for any possible movement. The wind changed directions. He thought he saw the faint outline of a person in front of the house and said, "What's that?"

"Still can't see a thing, Nate."

The wind changed directions again, and both men saw a figure by the horses. "That's the guy that fell into the front door, Nate!"

"Then shoot him!"

"It's too late. He's between the horses."

Nate ran from his position and yelled at Will who was still at the south end of the house. "Ray's out. He's got a horse!"

Will bolted to the back of the house yelling, "Go Titus! Go! Ray's out! Get Gunny! After Will saw Titus sprinting to the back door with the rest of the crew behind him, he yelled, "Miles! Ray's getting away by the horses! Leave Lucky and go!"

Miles dropped Lucky's reins and rode behind the north side of the house to where the horses were tied. He saw a horse in the distance on the narrow trail that ran northwest from the house and kicked Chipper's sides with his heels.

Titus blew open the back door. Smoke consumed the inside of the house. Titus ran up the stairs holding his right arm around his nose. He reached the top and yelled, "Gunny!" He heard a muffled sound in the room next to the staircase, went down to his hands and knees, and crawled to avoid the smoke as best he could. He saw Gunny tied to a wooden chair on the floor. Gunny tried desperately to keep his face on the floor to avoid breathing smoke. Titus quickly positioned the chair face up and pulled the top of the chair back with Gunny still tied to it as fast as he could down the stairs. The back chair legs broke off as they hit the stairs. Neither man could take a breath, but Titus kept pulling Gunny until he reached the back door frame. With one last pull, Titus and Gunny fell out of the house onto the ground. Michael cut Gunny's ropes while the rest of the crew ran to save Mirage and the rest of the gang's horses.

On the trail leading northwest from the house, Chipper quickly closed the distance to Ray's horse. No one would be riding off the trail here because the woods were too dense. Ray looked back and saw the morning sun outlining Chipper's chestnut and white colors and Miles out of the saddle leaning over Chipper's withers. Ray held the reins in one hand and pulled his pistol with the other. He looked back to aim it at Miles, but a small animal next to the trail felt the horse coming and rustled the leaves. Ray's horse suddenly boogered to the left, and he had to drop the pistol in order to grab the saddle horn. Miles saw Ray's flailing movements. Then he saw Ray's gun hit the ground. Ray repeatedly whipped the reins and kicked, but his horse could not outrun Chipper.

Will was on the same trail now with Lucky riding as fast as he could, but he still saw no one in front of him. As Miles closed the distance, he saw that Ray had both hands on his reins and kept glancing back. Miles waited until Ray looked forward again before he kicked. Then Chipper's mane blew back as he bolted to the left side of Ray's horse. Miles reached for *his* father's sword, and as Ray turned back again to look at Miles, he saw the sword raised above him on his left side. He instantly shifted all his weight and pulled his horse to the right. Miles brought the sword down as hard as he could. Ray's sudden move to the right, though, forced Miles to lean too far out of his saddle. His sword hit Ray's left rein and severed it, but Miles lost his grip and the sword fell to the ground.

Ray's hold on his horse was only with the right rein, so his horse turned toward a tree off the trail and stopped before hitting it. Ray became un-horsed and was thrown forward, over his saddle horn, and into the tree. The middle of Ray's back hit the tree first. It took him a couple of seconds, but he was still able to stand up and face Miles.

Miles spotted a hard old tree branch on the ground that was about four feet long. This was all he wanted. He dismounted Chipper, picked up the branch, and walked toward Ray. "I'll take that money belt you're wearing."

Ray pulled a large knife from the sheath on his belt. As Miles walked closer, he saw the gash on Miles right cheek together with the blood on his clothes and said, "Guess you met Wyrick – huh, honker?"

"You used that young man, Ray."

"He knew what he was getting into."

"He was just a kid. He didn't need to die! You and your *dead* brother should have sent him back where he came from."

Ray's eyes widened. Then his face turned an apoplectic red as he lunged at Miles with his knife. Miles held the branch vertically with both hands at its ends and met the blade with the middle of the branch. Ray's expression quickly changed from anger to fear. Then Miles took two steps toward Ray and kicked him in the crotch with his right foot. Ray fell to his knees and dropped the knife. Miles looked stoically down at Ray as he moved both hands to the end of the branch and swung it like a bat into Ray's forehead. The blow sent the back of Ray's head into the tree behind him. Ray's body went limp and fell forward onto the ground. Miles dropped the branch – glanced back down the path and saw Will sitting on Lucky, but making no attempt to help him and said, "How long have you been here?"

"Long enough to see you didn't even need the sword you dropped back there. You've really become quite the street fighter, Miles. How many people did you say you've killed today?"

"Shut up, Will. How about *you* go fight someone with a knife in the dark, who's taller than you and half your age. Ray was nothing compared to that."

"Miles, I wanted to help with Ray here, but you killed him before I could get off my horse! To hell with your sword – all you needed to beat this guy was a stick!"

"Very funny, Will. Now get your money belt off Ray's body because I'm not doing it."

Back at the *Cypress Queen*, Captain Bridges asked, "Are we finished with the repairs to the bow?"

One of the remaining crew said, "Aye Captain, the paddle wheel is fixed too. I think we can load."

"All right. The horses go on last – skittish ones dead last so they don't spook all the rest."

Captain Bridges made his way up to the pilothouse again. He was not happy. This trip down the Ohio River had turned into a disaster. He figured he had lost six crew members including his nephew and four passengers, one of which was personally committed to paying for boat's trip to St. Louis.

Then one of his men on the riverbank shouted, "Captain Bridges – I think you should see this!"

Captain Bridges was about to walk into the pilothouse, but turned around to see a long line of men and horses coming down the path to the boat led by Gunny riding Mirage – bareback with Titus right behind him on Clyde McConnell's other horse. Behind them was the rest of the crew riding an assortment of horses that he had never seen, followed by Will, Miles, Nate and Ian. As they drew closer, he could see that Gunny had been beaten, but he was alive and that was all that mattered.

Sarah saw the line of horses coming toward the *Cypress Queen* and ran to find Abigail who was coming out of one of the rooms on the boiler deck. "Abigail! They're back! Nate's alright!"

Abigail screamed "Caleb!" and ran down the staircase to the main deck and off the boat. Caleb ran out of their room to catch her. She kept running past all the other men and horses to Nate. "Nathaniel, you did it! – I have never been so worried in my life."

Nate hopped off Dominick and hugged her. Caleb ran to Nate's right leg. Nate picked Caleb up – held him over his head and said, "It wasn't easy Abby, but we did it. We all did it."

Peerless walked out of the pilothouse and saw the captain looking over the scene in silence. "Captain – they're back!"

A tear ran down Captain Bridges' right cheek. He watched the procession of horses and men below him, then slowly rubbed his cheek with his sleeve. "Yes, Peerless. They actually did it. Now, get us to St. Louis."

CHAPTER THIRTEEN
THE GREAT INLAND PORT

All the passengers and horses loaded before sunset and the *Cypress Queen* was underway again and traveling down the Ohio River. The men that came back from the woods had not slept for almost two days. Nevertheless, Captain Bridges heard a great deal of shouting and music below. He went down to the main deck and saw that Clyde McConnell was the fiddler for everyone celebrating the end of the Little gang.

When Captain Bridges joined the party, Ian had pushed Miles forward into Michael with a hard slap on the back and yelled, "Pass the whisky!" Miles, in turn, grabbed a bottle that was going by him. He took a swig first and gave it to Ian who took another long swig, rubbed his mouth with his shirt sleeve and shouted in a slurred Scottish brogue for all to hear, "Thanks, *Tree Stem!*"

Miles quickly said, "Ian, I really don't think anyone wants to hear–"

"Oh, I think they do." Then he shouted, "It was the damnedest thing I've ever seen – the way he took down that fiend in the dark – walking at him with nothing more than a forked twig!"

Will was ten feet away talking to Nate and Jacobus when he heard Ian describe the details of Miles' fight.

Hearing what really happened threw him into a coughing fit because he could not drink and laugh at the same time.

Nate slapped Will on the back in an effort to help him clear his throat and asked, "Did he say, *Tree Stem*?"

Will stopped coughing, cleared his throat as best he could and said in a raspy voice, "Yes, I'll explain later." Then he shouted, "If Miles is given the chance, he won't hesitate to go to the stick!" Once he saw he had everyone's attention, Will made a large sweeping gesture with his right hand holding the whisky bottle. "He prefers more of a natural killing these days with only an unfettered piece of wood. It's much less trouble than a sword, knife or gun!"

Ian, not to be outdone, yelled over everyone again, "Don't fight the man if he's anywhere near a forest!"

The crew members that were abused by the gang had tears in their eyes from laughing so hard.

Miles thought the jokes might go away sooner if he didn't respond, so he raised his hands and sarcastically said, "All right Ian – get it out of your system."

Captain Bridges made his way to Will, put his arm around him, and said, "Will, what happened out there?"

"Captain, Ian picked off about five of them in the front of the house before the rest of us came in the back door, but Titus had the biggest day of us all. That man's been bullwhipped and run at least two miles but killed two or three of their gang, mostly with his bare hands. He almost got shot off his horse, yet pulled Gunny out of a burning house all by himself."

Captain Bridges saw Titus enjoying himself with the others. "Thank God he and Gunny are alive. They are like sons to me."

"I almost know how you feel. We got to know them quickly on this trip."

Captain Bridges saw Titus and Gunny looking back at him and said, "Will you did it. Thank you. Now get some sleep. I have some crew members I have to talk to right now."

After almost two more days of travel down to Cairo and up the Mississippi, they started to see many more riverboats. When the *Cypress Queen* was three miles south of St. Louis, Gretchen and Sammy were at the bow and saw a lot of dark smoke ahead of them. Sammy said, "Look Mommy." Gretchen turned her head from another boat that was going down river and saw row after row of tall dark smokestacks protruding from the grayish white decks of at least a hundred steamboats. They were docked along the levee as far as she could see. There were large mounds of stacked freight, wagons and horses moving back and forth along the levee. People shouting, whistles, fiddlers, horns and horses could all be heard from a distance. The sheer amount of black smoke from all the smokestacks gathered for a moment and completely obscured their view of the levee until the wind blew in a different direction.

As the Cypress Queen merged into the boat traffic, the faint whine of a lone bagpiper's chanter and deep drones emanated from the docks. Ian somehow distinguished these sounds from all the others and awoke from his whisky induced sleep – opened his right eye and said, "We're here."

Will was in Captain's Bridges quarters to pay for their trip from Kentucky. They sat opposite each other in comfortable chairs with a small polished wooden table between them. On the table was a pot of coffee and two cups. Will was still tired from the past couple of days, but he was very upbeat. Captain Bridges poured him a cup of coffee and asked, "What's the line that's taking you up the

Missouri River to Westport?"

"Western Star."

"Western Star? I think that line was sold not too long ago."

"What do you mean sold?"

"New ownership Will – that's all."

"I have a contract with those people to travel to West Port, Captain. That's hundreds of miles up the Missouri River!"

"I'd take you to West Port if I could, but I can't. We take on freight here that has to go back up the Ohio. Besides, I don't have a Missouri River pilot even if I could do it."

"So all the money I paid up front to Western Star could all be gone?"

Captain Bridges set his cup down on the table and leaned forward. "I know what you're thinking, Will. You and your friends are going to be all right – come on." Captain Bridges stood up, walked to his door and motioned for Will to follow. They went into the pilothouse where Peerless looked for an area that would be best to unload the horses. "Peerless, get us as close as you can to Western Star's area."

"Aye Captain." The boat continued three quarters of a mile up the levee before Peerless said "This is where they've been Captain."

"All right Peerless, let's get to the best place to unload all their livestock and wagons."

The boat began a very slow turn to its larboard side. Peerless, Captain Bridges and Will saw another sternwheeler similar to the *Cypress Queen*, but this boat was larger and much newer. "Captain Bridges looked up at the metal letters *HGM* welded on the top spacer bar between the tall black smokestacks and said, "I haven't seen those letters on a boat before – must be a new line."

"The name plate under the pilothouse says *Empire Lander*. Is this our boat?"

"I don't know, Will, but I'll find out as soon as we dock."

As they continued to move slowly past, Captain Bridges saw more activity at its bow. He walked out of the pilothouse to the rail of the hurricane deck.

Will followed him. "What's wrong?"

Captain Bridges pointed at men who were fighting around the capstan behind the bow.

"It looks like they're having fun, Captain – just fists."

"It hasn't really started yet, Will – look." Captain Bridges pointed at a very muscular shirtless man over six-and-a-half feet tall with a shaved head and tattoos that covered his chest, back and arms. Compared to the others on deck, he was a giant. He had been leaning against a post with his arms crossed – simply watching the fight.

"Who's that?"

"That man is the ex-convict Brewton Lynch. He's known on this river as Hannibal Lynch. This fight is not going to end well for one of those men down there."

After watching the fight for a few seconds, something made Hannibal decide to walk directly into it. Several men in the middle of the fight were throwing punches at each other. One of the men was pushed back from the center and accidentally backed into Hannibal who appeared mildly irritated. He backhanded the man on his left ear as if he were swatting an insect. The man never saw the blow coming and fell to the deck unconscious. Hannibal continued to walk past him and reached for another one of the fighters that seemed to be beating the others. He grabbed the back of this man's collar with his right hand and the man's belt with his left. Then he lifted the man above his head, walked to the larboard side of the boat, away from the dock, and threw him into the river. After that, Hannibal noticed the *Cypress Queen* going past them. The small wake from its low speed rocked the *Empire Lander*. Hannibal walked slowly back to the others as the boat bobbed up and down. With both hands resting on his waist, he stared at Captain Bridges until the *Cypress Queen* passed. Then he turned his head and yelled, "Get him out of here!" The other men that were in the fight picked up the unconscious body of the man lying on the deck and took him off the boat.

The man who was thrown into the water swam to another part of the dock. Hannibal walked off the gang plank to him, bent down with his hand extended, and said "What is your name?"

"Jason Winship," said the soaked crewman.

Once the *Cypress Queen* was past the *Empire Lander*, Will asked "Captain, what was that all about?"

"The result of the fight was never in doubt, Will. The fortunate man was the one Hannibal threw headlong into the river."

"Fortunate?"

"Yes, Hannibal perceived him to be the strongest, so he'll be the second mate. The other man that was knocked senseless was losing the fight, so he will not be part of the crew because Hannibal perceived him to be the weakest."

"What a way to pick a crew."

"That's the way some boats do it, Will, but that doesn't matter. I need to find the clerk of the line and see what's going on. Hopefully they've got one on that boat."

"All we want to do is get to West Port without having to spend half a month at this levee waiting for another boat."

"I hear you. Let me see what I can find out when we

dock. It may be best if I go alone right now though, but I will help you Will."

After the Cypress Queen was moored, Captain Bridges walked onto the gangplank of the Empire Lander. He saw that Hannibal was still at the bow.

When Hannibal saw Captain Bridges, he glared at first, then smiled and spoke in a deep bellicose voice, "Well, if it isn't Captain Lane Bridges. Come aboard."

Captain Bridges had dealt with Hannibal before and knew he could be a smooth talker. He mocked his cordiality because he knew it wasn't true. "Hannibal, how perfectly gracious of you."

Hannibal frowned for a split second then quickly smiled again. "Why Captain, I don't go by the nickname of my home town in Missouri any longer. Please call me Brewton."

Captain Bridges ignored his pretend smile and appearance in order find out more information. "All right Brewton – I would like to meet your captain and agent."

"The captain isn't here right now, but the agent is. Let me get him for you."

With that, Hannibal turned and climbed the staircase behind them to the boiler deck. After two minutes, a short slender young man with dark hair combed back, and wearing a white shirt with a tight dark vest walked down the stairs to the main deck. He carried a clipboard in his left hand and had a pencil resting on his right ear. When he reached Captain Bridges, he extended his right hand and said in a high voice, "Hello I'm Harvey Pennington, agent for HGM. May I help you?"

Captain Bridges shook his hand. "Yes I'm Lane Bridges, captain of the *Cypress Queen*. We came from Kentucky with passengers and livestock on their way to West Port. Is it true that all the Western Star boats have been sold?"

The nattily dressed clerk said, "Yes Captain, we have assumed all the holdings of Western Star and have been expecting these passengers for some time now. I'm glad you arrived because I was actually getting ready to book their places."

"We had a delay on the Ohio River, but they are here now and ready–"

The clerk abruptly said, "Very well Captain – their Western Star contract will be honored. Have them board as soon as they can and be ready for departure first thing in the morning."

Captain Bridges frowned. "So *this* is the HGM boat that will be taking them?

"Yes Captain."

"And who is the Captain? I want to see him."

"I'm sorry, but Captain Hammermill is indisposed at the moment."

"Chet Hammermill?"

"Yes, do you know him?"

"Know of him is more like it." Captain Bridges' demeanor became more serious. He looked up toward the pilothouse to spot the captain or anyone else. Not seeing anyone, he turned and walked away.

Harvey pursed his lips, pulled his shoulders back and tried to sound authoritative. "I am sure he will be very sorry he missed you too Captain and I will, of course, extend to him your words."

"Indisposed?" Captain Bridges scoffed. "Goodbye Mr. Pennington." Then he walked down the gangplank.

Harvey, happy that the conversation was over, looked left and right – then began to scurry back up to his office. After grabbing the handrail and taking two steps, though, he saw Hannibal waiting for him at the top of the staircase.

Hannibal looked down. "He's indisposed? I will extend to him your words? You blithering little vest pocket! Get to Hammermill's quarters now."

After hearing a rap on his door, the words, "Come in Hannibal" were uttered from a faint voice. Hannibal carefully poked his head in the door because he wasn't sure what to expect inside. He saw Captain Hammermill sitting on his bed reading a book with a small glass of whiskey on his night stand.

Captain Hammermill said, "Well?" in a slurred voice.

Hannibal entered the doorway, being careful to duck his head, with Harvey right behind him. "I think Bridges almost believed it until this little idiot's last sentence. We will be lucky if they get on the boat in the morning."

"I was trying to sound formal!" said Harvey.

Hannibal motioned for the Captain to move from his own bed. Captain Hammermill stood and took three clumsy steps to his desk chair. He attempted to sit quickly into the seat but missed. An "EEYAAH!" followed as the wooden chair arm hit him between the legs. He slowly moved his rear end backwards into the seat, then lowered his face into his hands on the desk while he waited for the pain to go away.

Hannibal reclined with his head on the Captain's pillow. His feet hung off the foot of the bed and almost touched the floor. He was silent for a few moments after the Captain's attempt to sit and simply stared at the ceiling. "Harvey, don't show your face again on this voyage."

Harvey's cheeks flushed, and he raised his voice a little higher than usual. "I...have done exactly as I was told, and *you* know it! You...engraved peacock!"

Hannibal, still looking at the ceiling, said in a deep monotone voice, "That's it – leave – go back to your office or get off the boat – just go away – you've done enough."

Harvey laid his clipboard and pen on the Captain's small bed side table very precisely, then took off his fitted vest – threw it at Hannibal's face and chirped, "Fine! I'll be going back to the restaurant." Then he slammed the door on his way out.

Hannibal slowly lifted the vest with his right hand and dropped it off the side of the bed.

Captain Hammermill, with his face still resting in his hands, said, "Will they board?"

Hannibal paused for a moment and replied, "From the way I read Bridges, they are motivated to get to West Port, so I say we are leaving with them in the morning despite that little fop. If that happens, you will have to make some sort of an appearance."

A muffled "All right Hannibal – let me know" came from between Captain Hammermill's hands.

Will saw Captain Bridges walking intently up the dock toward the *Cypress Queen* and said "What's wrong?"

"I'll tell you what's wrong! You have a boat – but the captain, if you can call him that – has been fired from at least two steamboat lines for dereliction of duty and drunkenness. He was almost convicted a few years ago for ordering his boat to leave a dock despite having boiler problems. His actions led to an explosion that killed an engineer. I can't believe another line would hire him!"

"Did you talk to him?"

"No, they covered for him. I think he was hiding."

Will thought for a few seconds and stated, "I've been around a lot of drunks. Some of them aren't half bad. What if a drunk captain's all we've got?"

"If Chet Hammermill *is* the Captain, he's not really in charge. That's why I don't understand the presence of Hannibal. No line or captain in their right mind would hire him as their first mate with his history."

"Will was silent at first, then shrugged. "No offense, but what does it matter what the captain does if Hannibal and the pilots can get us to West Port?"

Captain Bridges looked at Will and laughed. "Captains *and cowboys* are not all the same, Will. Do what you want, but remember that Hannibal is not to be trusted. Watch out for him. Keep your guns with you. Never give them up. Get to know the crew working under that criminal, and if you can, get to know the pilots."

Will nodded. "All we want to do is–"

"I know Will. I assumed you'd go. You guys aren't the typical passengers we carry on these boats – especially after seeing what you did to that gang on the Ohio."

"We couldn't have done it without Titus."

"I must admit I was a little keyed up when I first met you."

"I had misgivings at first, too, Captain. Then Gunny told me about your child. I've thought about what that must have been like for you. You must know there are many bad things that can happen in life, but *your* life has just as much meaning as his did. Every day you are here is important for the lives that you touch – especially Titus and Gunny."

Captain Bridges eyes welled up, and he did his best not to become emotional. "It has been an honor, Will Richards. The best of luck to you."

Will put his right hand on the Captain's back. "Same to you, Captain. I hope we see each other again."

After that, Will walked toward Miles and the others on the main deck then said, "All right guys, let's move."

CHAPTER FOURTEEN
THE BIG MUDDY

The sun rose on the *Empire Lander*, and the St. Louis wharf came back to life with the sounds of steamboats readying themselves for departure. Their eventual travels would reach as far as New Orleans, St. Paul, Pittsburg and Fort Union. The crew was still awaiting the boarding of everyone from the *Cypress Queen*. Hannibal exited his quarters to make his way down from the hurricane deck, but hit his forehead on the doorframe. He quietly cursed and rubbed the top of his head, then walked to the railing and saw Harvey standing at the dock with a suitcase.

He made his way down to the gangplank and glibly asked, "Harvey, I thought you quit?"

Harvey, now assuming a resolute tone, announced, "Hannibal, we must talk. Come here."

Hannibal walked out the gangplank to the dock. "What could we possibly *have* to talk about after that little fit you pitched yesterday?"

"You still need me Hannibal to make it work."

A cynical smile came across Hannibal's face. "All right Harvey, I'm listening."

"Who else do you have to sell this other than that drunk?"

"What do you mean?"

"Think about it, Hannibal. Is the prestige of this steamboat line really going to be reflected by just you and that loose collection of human intelligence you call deckhands?"

"They will do what I tell them."

"I'm a waiter, and I know more about this boat than half those guys. Also, take a look at yourself and that new knot on your forehead. People see you and want to run the other way."

Hannibal grinned. "That hurts, Harvey. I don't know how I'm going get past your low opinion of me."

"I'm not kidding, Hannibal. How are you *alone* going to get Richards to trust you if he sees that no one else trusts you?"

Hannibal stopped smiling. "You talk way too much, but you may have a point."

"Look Hannibal, my presence here is a far better idea than *you* parading around with all those needless cries for attention etched all over your body. We both want to make something on this – right?"

Hannibal looked down the dock – then looked back up at Harvey. "Okay, but from now on, you will be known as the *Agent of the Line* instead of the clerk. That sounds better anyway."

Harvey heard the clopping of hoofs on the dock. He looked to the east, shielded his eyes from the sun, and saw Will Richards leading a procession of horses and people toward the *Empire Lander*.

Hannibal leaned down and whispered, "Okay, it's time to go to work. Don't oversell it, twit."

"Twit? I'm not the utter lummox that keeps hitting his head on door frames. Now take my bag to the office – get the boat ready to go, and I'll show them aboard."

As Will approached the *Empire Lander*, Harvey met him at the top of the gangplank. He held out his hand, smiled and said pretentiously, "I presume you are Mr.

Richards from Kentucky. I am Harvey Pennington, agent of the new HGM line. Welcome aboard."

Will, after thinking about Captain Bridges' warnings, simply said, "Thank you Mr. Pennington. I assume we load the horses and freight first?"

"Yes Mr. Richards, but we also have other passengers and freight that are not part of your group from the *Cypress Queen.*"

"Why?"

"This is a larger boat than you originally hired, Mr. Richards. We are honoring your original contract, but pursuant to the purchase and sale agreement with the previous owner, HGM is still allowed to maximize the capacity of this boat."

Will thought that was what happened and didn't really care. The only thing that mattered to him, at this point, was that they were not stranded at the St. Louis levee. "I understand, Harvey, but the women and children will continue to have their rooms on the boiler deck right?"

"Yes, no travel arrangements have changed, but more women and children outside of your party will be occupying the boiler deck."

"All right Harvey, we'll load our horses if you don't mind."

Harvey quickly said, "Of course Mr. Richards" and turned to greet the rest of the people from George Town, as they came aboard.

Miles was right behind Will and quietly said, "I thought we were supposed to be on a Western Star boat?"

Will took in a breath and raised his eyebrows. "Miles, just thank the lord that we have a boat *at all* right now."

"So there was a problem?"

"I handled it. Everything's fine."

"What happened?"

"Western Star went belly up after I hired them. We got lucky."

"I should've known. Whenever you're not irritating me, there's always something wrong."

After all the passengers and freight were on board, Will walked toward the bow. Hannibal was ordering the crew to stack wood in certain areas. He saw Will and extended his hand as he walked toward him. "Hello, I'm Brewton Lynch, first mate of the *Empire Lander*."

Will shook his hand. "Yes, I'm Will Richards – Captain Bridges said I should meet you, but he called you Hannibal."

"He is a fine captain, Will. When I first started working on the rivers, the mates and captains called me Hannibal because that's where I grew up in Missouri."

"You like the body art. What made you get so many?"

"It all started when I was a very young man. Each one had a particular meaning in my life that was important to me at that time. Surely you have had moments in your life that you wanted to preserve as well."

"Yes, but I didn't put them all over my body."

"I hope you still preserved the important ones in some way. We only live once. On this journey you might find something worth keeping like I have."

"I've got lot of things I want to keep, but right now I would like to meet the captain."

"I'm sorry, but he has asked not to be disturbed because he is working on the business of this new steamboat line. He has goals he must meet in freight and passengers over the next few months. This is his first voyage on the new line. I'm sure you understand."

"May I meet the pilots then?"

"We only have one pilot on this trip. Let's get past the confluence of the Missouri River, and I will take you up.

Excuse me now though. I have to speak with the engineer."

Miles was standing by the horses during Will's conversation. When he saw Hannibal leave, he went to the bow and, in a low voice asked, "Who's that big character with all the tattoos?"

Will looked around to make sure Hannibal was gone and quietly answered, "That's Brewton Lynch, the first mate. They call him Hannibal."

"He's one of the meanest looking people I've ever seen. He looks like he just got out of prison."

"You can't judge everyone by their appearance, Miles. He's well spoken and seems to have a nice heart. If he had a rough life, he could have reformed. Give him a chance."

"Whatever – he's got a look in his eye I don't like. I'm not trusting the guy. Now come back here and help us shovel after these horses."

As Will followed Miles to the horses he said, "What happened to the kind innocent unassuming Miles I used to know? I think having to kill those people back there has soured you against your fellow man."

"I'm not shoveling after your horse, Will. Sleep in manure if you want."

Ian was also shoveling muck next to Chipper and said, "Are you talking about that ink-blotted goon!"

Will whispered, "Ian, come on, lower your voice."

Miles stopped shoveling and looked at Ian. "The guy is Will's new friend now, and *we* are being too judgmental."

Ian raised his voice. "There's nothing wrong with judging people, Will. You're an idiot! That goon would sell his own mother for twenty dollars."

Miles laughed.

Will motioned with his arms and hands for Ian and Miles to lower their voices. Then he looked over his shoulder again to see if Hannibal was still nearby. "Come on Ian. He's going to hear you!"

Miles took a breath. "Yeah, I bet his jail guard thought he was largely misunderstood too."

Ian, also laughing, raised his voice again. "I'm sorry sir – we can't help you today. Your last ass tattoo used up all our ink!"

Will shook his head in disgust. "You sound like a bunch of morons." Then he walked between them to pick up a shovel at the other end of the main deck.

After the St. Louis levee was behind them, Hannibal approached the door to Harvey's office. It had an opaque pane of glass framed on the upper half of the door. He didn't knock, but did remember to duck his head as he entered the small workspace. He noticed Harvey sitting behind his desk, and on the other side, there stood a chair that looked like it was made for a child.

Hannibal carefully lowered his body onto the chair without breaking it, then looked at Harvey and started to speak, but Harvey cut him off. "Hammermill can't hide up there the whole time. He needs to do something or they're going to get suspicious."

"Will already asked to see him and meet the pilot."

Harvey frowned. "That's Bridges' doing, so he obviously never trusted you. You need to be present when Will meets *our* pilot because he is the only one that can screw this up and, from what I see, he doesn't trust you either."

"I'm still working on Will."

"Don't overdo it...wait... another thing...when we speak, or you talk to Hammermill, or that pilot – keep the conversation only between you and whoever you are talking to. You cannot be overheard. That goes for these things you shout into all over this boat."

"They are called speaking tubes."

"I don't care what they're called or how you do it, but your conversations must be private. No passenger can hear you!"

Hannibal looked around Harvey's modest work area and said, "You need to get out of this closet and talk to the rest of the passengers."

"*You* need to focus on getting Hammermill presentable, and while you're at it, you may want to put on a shirt."

Hannibal curled his lip and rose from the Lilliputian chair. He poked his head out of Harvey's office door to see if anyone could have heard them talking. Seeing no one, he ducked his head, stepped out of the office, and gently shut Harvey's door behind him.

Martin Clearman saw Hannibal coming down the stairs from Harvey's office. Then he saw Will on the main deck and said, "Why haven't we seen the captain yet?"

"The first mate told me the captain is catching up on paperwork because they're part of a new steamboat line now."

"That's normally the agent's job, Will, but for some reason that guy has been spending all his time with the first mate."

"I'll go meet the pilot then Martin. It looks like this boat only has one, so maybe I can find out more up there."

"If there's just one, we won't be traveling at night. Let me know. I've been watching the rest of this crew too. They're very green."

When Will made his way up to the pilothouse, Hannibal happened to be standing in front of it's door with a smile on his face. "Will, I was coming to get you. Would you like to meet the pilot now?"

"That's why I'm here."

"I must tell you, Will, not all boats have the same rules. Here at HGM, passengers are not allowed on the hurricane deck unless they are with the captain or the first mate."

"Good – I'm glad you're here. Let's go."

"I'm always happy to take you to the pilot, or the captain whenever you like, Will. It's a rule I have to follow as well."

"You've made your point."

Without letting his smile go, Hannibal opened the door to the pilothouse. "Travis, this is Will Richards. He is with the group from Kentucky."

The pilot kept his eyes on the river in front of him. He was a man of average height in his early thirties with red hair and the beginnings of a beard. "Hi Will, I'm Travis Wheeler."

"I've never been up the Missouri River, Travis. I hear it can be tricky."

"That's right. All rivers change, but this one changes *very* quickly depending on the weather, and from the way those clouds look over there, we are about to get some."

Will pointed at a part of the current from the Missouri River coming closest to them. "Look at the dirt that river is carrying."

"They call it the Big Muddy, Will. It's an alluvial river. Every year, the tons of washed out earth this river brings to the Mississippi numbers in the hundreds of millions."

"So it's the amount of flooding that makes the river flow so differently?"

"That and the soil."

"How long is the trip to West Port?"

"It can be a couple of nights or longer depending on the conditions *if* we were traveling at night. This trip, though, I'm the only pilot, so we won't be traveling at night."

"So how long do you think?"

"It's hard to say. Snags are really bad on this river. Trees get washed off their banks all the time. Their trunks bottom out and point down river – right at us, so they can be very hard to see especially if they're under the water line; and, if we get weather like what we're seeing now, it's even more difficult."

"Four days?"

"I just can't say exactly, Will, but it shouldn't be more than a three or four days if we're lucky and don't see any bars."

"Thanks Travis. What's the captain's experience on this river?"

"You'll have to ask him, Will. I haven't seen him yet."

Hannibal's eyes widened. He became so infuriated with Travis' reply that he started to shake, but he controlled himself and calmly said, "I can assure you Will, Captain Hammermill has a lot of experience on this river from a variety of boats. You will be able to talk to him yourself at dinner tonight in his quarters."

"Great, I look forward to meeting him, Hannibal."

"He looks forward to meeting you as well. Would you like to meet the engineer?"

"Sure. Let's go."

Will walked out of the pilothouse. Hannibal didn't immediately follow Will out the door but instead glared at Travis.

Travis smirked. "Come back anytime, Hannibal. I love our little visits."

Hannibal reached for Travis' right arm, but he heard Will shout, "Hannibal, come on!"

Hannibal slowly lowered his hand and said, "Continue remarks like that, *driver*, and this will be your last job."

Gray clouds continued to form around them and rain gently fell. Will followed Hannibal down to the engine room. There, they saw a gruff man with a white beard and clad in an undershirt. He was busy telling two young crewmen where and how to stack fire wood. Hannibal said, "Will, this is Mr. Seagraves, our engineer."

Will extended his hand. "Hi I'm Will—"

Before they could shake, a bell rang. Mr. Seagraves adjusted the throttle valve, and the engines slowed.

Hannibal reached for the speaking tube to the pilothouse and shouted, "Travis! What is it?"

Travis calmly replied, "It's starting to rain."

Hannibal looked at Will and Mr. Seagraves and said, "Something upstairs needs my attention. Please excuse me for a moment." Then he walked out of the engine room and ran up the stairs trying not to hit his head on a beam. He finally reached the hurricane deck, burst into the pilothouse and yelled, "Rain?"

Travis, with his hands still on the wheel guiding the boat to shore, said, "That's right – rain – I can't *see* the river."

"I can see the river. It's right there! What do you mean you can't see the river?"

"I'm not able to read it. The rain hitting the water makes everything look the same. There's no telltale sign of water rushing around something like a snag. It's too dangerous right now."

Hannibal paused to take a breath. "How long...do you want to sit here then, Travis?"

"Until it stops raining, or dawn if it rains past dark, then I'll just have to see."

Hannibal yelled, "We sit here till it stops raining?"

"I haven't been on this river in weeks. We never got a report from the last boat that came down it to tell us what to look out for. When you guys hired us, you said *we* leave in the morning, period!"

Hannibal fumed, "We'll never make West Port at this rate!"

"Then pilot it yourself, Hannibal! I'm going to my quarters as soon as we tie up."

Hannibal grabbed Travis' right wrist and squeezed it. "Do you even know who I am?"

"Yes, a soon to be stranded first mate with no pilot and no captain on the Missouri River."

A familiar high voice at the door to the pilothouse broke in. "I thought I would find you here. Let him go before all of our passengers with guns decide to come up here and ask questions you can't answer, you shortsighted fool."

Hannibal looked at Harvey standing in the doorway, then sneered at Travis. "You and I will meet again after we reach West Port."

After Hannibal left, Travis saw the speaking tube leading to the main deck and smiled, then he reached down and subtly disconnected it.

That night, Hannibal came to meet Will on the main deck before dinner with the Captain. Will saw he was wearing a shirt and said, "Hannibal, I didn't know we were dressing up. I would have worn my jacket."

"I know – I've heard it before, Will. For me, though, it gets hot working on these boats at times. I hate to feel sweat on my clothes, that's all. Come with me. The captain is waiting for us."

Will followed Hannibal to the hurricane deck. The captain's door was open and they walked inside. Captain Hammermill stood up. He was wearing a pressed uniform, dark tie and shined shoes. The uniform, though, was either too big or the captain had lost weight.

He reached out his hand to Will and said, "Welcome to the Empire Lander."

"It's a pleasure to finally meet you, Captain."

Hammermill stammered, "Well yes...I mean...I'm glad to meet you as well, William."

"Call me Will, Captain."

The Captain stood as erect as possible. "Yes, of course Will...come in and sit down."

Will watched the captain, Hannibal and Harvey take a seat around a table that had obviously been brought in for this occasion because it was too large for the size of the room.

As soon as Will sat, crew members brought in four large bowls of beef stew and quickly placed them in front of each man with a glass of water for each.

Will exclaimed, "This may be the best meal I've had since leaving George Town, Captain."

Captain Hammermill leaned back in his chair. "Eat up William – enjoy."

"Captain, why are we stopped?"

"Stopped? Oh...well – safety! Yes, William, the safety of every man, woman and child aboard and, *by dint of great*, we shall overcome!"

"By what?"

Harvey glared at Hannibal.

Hannibal quickly said, "What Captain Hammermill means is–"

Will looked past Captain Hammermill at the half empty bottle of whisky behind him on the desk. "I think I understand, Hannibal."

The captain's hand shook as he lifted a spoonful of stew to his mouth, but as soon as he tried to swallow, he coughed and gasped for air.

Harvey removed the spoon from his mouth and cried

out, "Hannibal, he's choking."

Hannibal jumped from his seat and got behind the captain. Will quickly stood and pushed his chair back. Hannibal placed his arms under the captain's ribcage and yanked several times. Finally, a small piece of meat came out of the captain's mouth and hit the middle of the table in front of them. Then the captain began another series of gasps, which led to a coughing fit and a slight regurgitation of the stew.

Hannibal wiped his mouth and picked him up like a child, then gently placed him on his bed with a pillow behind his head. After a few moments, he turned to Will and said, "I'm sorry, but I think dinner is over."

"Damn Hannibal – he almost choked to death right in front of us! Are you sure he's okay?"

"Yes Will. He just needs some rest now."

"Okay – glad he's breathing. Stay with him. I'm sorry Hannibal. I'll see you tomorrow I guess..." As Will left he thought, *Shit, Bridges was right.*

With the Captain's door shut, Hannibal sat back in his chair at the table and sighed. After a few moments, he reached for the captain's whiskey – took a large swig and passed the bottle to Harvey. Instead of taking a swig directly from the bottle, however, Harvey poured a small amount of whisky in the bottom of his glass. After that, he sat back in his chair, crossed his legs and quipped, "That went well – don't you think?"

Hannibal reached for the bottle again and looked at Captain Hammermill breathing in an almost fetal position on the bed with his face to the wall. "Perhaps there will be another chance for him to act like a captain."

Harvey took a sip. "Oh my god...Hannibal, you must be kidding! The old man almost died on us before the dessert."

CHAPTER FIFTEEN
WALKING THE BOAT

Will awoke to the familiar sounds of the paddles hitting the water. They disturbed the quiet morning, but for the passengers aboard the *Empire Lander*, the constant time and cadence of the paddles hitting the water were a soothing reminder that they were progressing again up the river.

Will tapped Miles' shoulder as he walked toward the front of the boat. Between the two large vertically mounted poles at the bow, he saw a curve in the river and a larger body of still water before curve. The way the sun cast its light on this body of water was reflective and disguised the water's true color. As the boat reached the curve, Will saw that the water changed its appearance from a muddy color to a deep red; and as the boat continued moving, it turned to a bright silver.

Miles followed Will to the bow and exclaimed, "That's incredible."

"I know, Miles, look at the willows and cottonwoods and the way the land frames the colors coming off the water."

Miles raised his right arm to be level with his chest and dramatically gestured with his right hand. "So, the mighty West begins right here."

"I always thought the West began in St. Louis when we started going up the Missouri, but if you see the West as beginning in this *very* spot, then I'm very happy for you

Miles."

Miles continued to gesture. "Land as far as you can see, both this way and that!"

Will left the bow and walked back to Lucky, but still spoke loud enough for Miles to hear, "Okay, smartass. That's the last time I try to show you anything."

The *Empire Lander* continued on its way for several more hours interrupted only for tree cutting stops.

Will didn't like the fact that they were dependent on steamboat crews instead of themselves. He wanted to know up front what he and his friends could be getting into before something else unexpected happened. He saw Hannibal checking something at the bow, and when he walked past again, Will asked, "It looks like this is going to be a meandering ride. How long till we get to West Port?"

Hannibal stopped. "Yes, from what I understand, there's no straight line between a beginning and an end on this river. The boat goes west, but only after going north and south first or wherever the lower elevations on the river take us. It's going to take time I think, but right now I've got to go to talk to the crew."

Will thought, *That, tells me absolutely nothing,* so he went up to the boiler deck to visit with the rest of the people from George Town. Martin Clearman was at the rail watching the crew and the river. "Martin, how long do you think this is going to take?"

"Its hard to say. Right now the river is falling. That's why the mate's so anxious. They're going to have to start sounding in a little while."

"Sounding?"

"Letting the pilot know about the depth of the river in certain places. They'll probably use that little boat called a yawl hanging next to the captain's quarters – then measure the depth with a weighted rope."

"Who sounds?"

"It'll probably be the first mate on this boat. The rest of the crew don't know what they're doing."

A few more hours passed before they reached a point where the river became much lower. Hannibal attempted to use the speaking tube on the main deck to speak with Travis, but it didn't work and said, "Damn it," then hurriedly climbed the stairs to the pilothouse again.

Before Hannibal could ask a question, Travis turned his head away from the river and said to Hannibal, "It hasn't happened yet, but if it happens, it happens. Up ahead, though, we're going to sound for sure. See that area about two hundred yards away?"

Hannibal frowned, walked out of the pilothouse, and called certain crewmen to assist with the yawl. After another fifteen minutes, the stopping bell sounded, and the boat slowed. Travis yelled from the window of the pilothouse, "Okay Hannibal, give me some depths out there!" Hannibal grabbed a lead line and motioned for crew members to come with him. The crew boarded and paddled the yawl to a point of the river in front of the *Empire Lander*, and Hannibal shouted water depths to Travis. After half a mile of Hannibal methodically checking the depth of the water and Travis trying not ground the steamboat, the yawl came upon an area where the river narrowed. After another bend in the river, the crew members in the yawl stopped paddling and everyone on the *Empire Lander* heard the stopping bell again. Crew members walked toward the bow. No one spoke. They simply gazed at a sandbar that stretched almost fifty yards between them and the rest of the river leading west.

Hannibal came aboard from the yawl and attempted

to use the speaking tube on the main deck. The device still didn't work, so he hit the wall with the flat of his hand and shouted, "Goddamn it!" When he ran up the stairs this time, however, the toe of his left boot caught one of the steps, and he fell face first onto the stairs. Hannibal sat in the middle of the staircase for a brief moment to compose himself. Then he touched his hand to his nose and noticed he was bleeding. When Travis saw him at the door breathing heavily with a bloody nose, he said, "Hannibal, you need to be more careful with..."

"Driver! The goddamned speaking tube isn't working and..."

"Did you break it?"

"I haven't broken any..."

"You can fix it later because right now you're going to need to save your energy for sparring the boat for about fifty yards! Better let the old man know."

"Hannibal stood at the door for a few seconds starring at Travis, then slammed it and walked away.

Travis chuckled and quietly said, "Have fun with that...Numpty."

Hannibal barged into the captain's quarters and announced, "We've got to walk the boat."

Captain Hammermill frowned. "How far?"

"About fifty yards."

The captain raked his hand through his white hair and calmly muttered, "Well...shit."

"This crew is green, Chet. It's not going to be good."

"We're going to shore I take it?"

"Right now."

The backing bell sounded. Will saw Martin Clearman at the bow with a cup of coffee in his hands. "Martin, what's going on?"

"Don't ask."

"We're going to use those poles at the bow aren't we?

"Yes, but we're going to have to unload."

"Unload what?"

"Most everything."

"Jesus."

"You can't say things like that in vain. I thought you were converting – remember?"

"So, everything on the boat comes off?"

"Yes, and we have to move all of it past the bar."

Will pointed to an area almost seventy yards away. "Then reload everything way over there?"

"That's right. The load has to be lightened. No one ever wants to walk a boat, but this river has a mind of its own. There's enough water on the other side of the bar out there, but the river is only flowing on the narrow side on that bank off the larboard side. If we try to maneuver through that area, we could still get stuck and have to walk the boat even farther."

Will went back to Miles, Nate and Ian. "Gentlemen, we have work to do. We're evacuating the boat of almost everything we brought aboard."

Nate said, "That's going to take some time, Will."

"So, the sooner we begin, the better – right?"

Miles smirked. "So what – there's no fight to the death like we had on the last boat?"

Ian bellowed, "It's finally time for the goon to go to work. This ought to be good!"

When the boat moved backwards, Harvey poked his head out of his office and walked down the staircase to the main deck. He saw Hannibal and inquired, "What's going on now?"

"A lot of grueling and arduous work. Something you know nothing about."

"Good, let me know when it's over."

Hannibal watched him scoot away and said, "little twit" under his breath.

The boat made its way to the north bank of the river. Two crew members tied the bow and stern to cottonwood trees. Two more crew members positioned the starboard side gangplank while others told all the passengers to pack their belongings and prepare to go to the riverbank. For almost two hours, passengers and crew moved livestock, trunks and freight off the boat and up the riverbank to an area where they would be reloaded. The passengers decided to use their opportunity off the boat to also tour the area and stretch their legs. Many of them removed their boots and walked on the sandbar around the boat. Travis was finally satisfied with the *Empire Lander's* lighter draft in the water.

Captain Hammermill noticed that he didn't hear any more noises from below and walked out of his quarters to see what had happened. He saw Hannibal on the main deck ordering the strongest crew members to the bow and shouted like he was in command. "Hannibal, can those men you have at the bow do it?"

Hannibal fumed and ran up the stairs again. Hammermill no longer saw Hannibal on the main deck, so he assumed his first mate didn't hear the question and walked back to his quarters. Hannibal appeared on the hurricane deck and burst into Hammermill's cabin.

The captain sputtered, "What...what the hell?"

Hannibal spun him around and spoke in a low voice. "Chet, the *only* reason I came up here is because the passengers on the riverbank, that could still hear you, were *also* watching and listening to you yapping at me! I told you before what I thought. The crew is green, but they'll do it or die trying – we're not waiting for rain. Now stay in your quarters and shut up until we need you for something!"

Captain Hammermill's lower lip quivered as Hannibal slammed the door on his way out.

Travis rang the starting bell and the boat slowly moved to the narrowest part of the sandbar. Travis used the speaking tube to the engine room and enthusiastically said, "Mr. Seagraves! let's run her up a little. Keep the buckets in the water. We still have to give that oaf something to work with."

"All right, Travis, here it is." Mr. Seagraves applied a burst of steam. The paddle wheel churned water behind them until the bow was on the sandbar.

"Mr. Seagraves – you know this crew has never sparred a boat."

"If they botch it, Travis, we could be stuck on this bar for weeks."

"Thank God it's not a hundred yards."

"Small comfort, Travis."

Hannibal yelled, "The capstan bars! Now!"

Martin Clearman stood on the river bank closer to the boat and watched the activity at the bow. Will stood next to him and asked, "What are they doing now?"

"Those bars they are carrying go into the holes of the capstan, which looks like a spindle, but its function tightens the ropes. The men use the bars to wind the ropes around the capstan like yoked animals on a mill."

"Then the bow comes up?"

"Yep – the winding of the capstan will pull those ropes through the deck tackle; then, the bow of the boat will draw up to meet the tackle on top of the big wooden poles. The whole thing is kind of like the boat using crutches to drag itself across the bar."

Will saw several crewmen trying to position the spars

at angles to both sides of the bow.

Hannibal yelled, "Prepare the ropes!"

Crewmen positioned the ropes from the starboard and larboard sides of each spar to the capstan while several other crewmen began to push the bars as hard as they could. The capstan turned. The ropes tightened and the pulleys inside the blocks squeaked. The men turning the capstan, though, quickly reached their limit and struggled to turn it further.

Hannibal yelled, "Use your legs and push, you weak bastards!"

The crewmen leaned forward again into the bars and pushed as hard as they could. This time, they all leaned much lower to allow their legs to do more of the work. The capstan turned again, but one of the men lost his footing and fell to the deck.

Hannibal yelled, "Get up!"

The man that had fallen ripped his right pant leg. His right knee began to bleed, but he got back up and tried to push as best he could. The bow of the *Empire Lander* rose from the sandbar. Hannibal looked up at the pilothouse and waved his right arm in a circle.

Seeing Hannibal's gesture, Travis said into the speaking tube, "Mr. Seagraves now!"

The boilers were already hot and ready to deliver steam. The paddle wheel turned against the water. The bow rose off the sandbar to its apex between the spars and fell back down with a shudder. The men that were pushing the bars on the capstan fell to the deck. After all their efforts, the boat moved only a few yards.

Harvey had fallen asleep at his desk with his forehead resting on the back of his right hand. When the hull dropped to the sandbar, his head popped up, so he came out of his office to see what was happening.

Hannibal yelled, "Again – move!"

The crew at the bow slowly got up and loosened the rope on the capstan to do it all over again. After that, they repositioned the spars, but just as they all started pushing the bars, the crewman with the bleeding knee lost his footing again and fell to the deck. Hannibal grabbed a log from a stack of fire wood and walked to the bleeding crewman, who was now on his hands and knees trying to get up. Hannibal yelled "Get up!" The crewman didn't move fast enough for Hannibal, so he brought the log down hard on the crewman's back. He screamed and fell face forward onto the deck.

From the riverbank nearest the boat, Gretchen said, "Clyde, that man is horrible."

Clyde shouted at Will. "Hey, big man! Is that guy really your friend?"

Abigail was having none of it. She walked closer to the boat on the sandbar and yelled, "Hey, Hermann! You're the one who needs the beat-down, not him!"

Nate grabbed her arm and sternly said, "Abby, his name is Hannibal. I feel the same way you do, but we have to get to West Port. Right now, we're a hundred miles from nowhere, and they don't *have* to let us back on that boat."

Abby pulled her arm out of Nate's hand. "That man's no good, Nate. He has to be stopped."

"Okay Abby. I hear you, but we can't do anything standing here on the sand."

When Will saw what happened, he became furious inside but couldn't do anything about it either because he was so far away, so instead of yelling, he walked to his friend, looked him in the eye and said, "I'll handle it, Clyde."

Nate made his way to Will and argued. "We cannot

allow this kind of cruelty to stand. Who is in charge of this boat anyway?"

"Nate, I said I'll handle it, but I can't do anything right now."

Travis also saw Hannibal beat the defenseless crewman and shouted into the speaking tube, "Mr. Seagraves – put some water under this hull and see what that oaf does!" Then Travis rang the backing bell.

"Aye, Travis. Give the ass a quick lesson!"

Hannibal heard the backing bell and became livid. He looked behind him and glared up at Travis in the pilothouse. The paddle wheel turned backwards and churned water up and under the hull. Hannibal threw the log onto the deck and yelled at the men at the capstan, "Keep us moving forward. I'll be right back." He ran up the stairs cursing. When he reached the door of the pilothouse, he jerked it open – got within inches of Travis' face and yelled, "What the hell are you doing, driver? You saw me getting those scrubs to move this boat forward didn't you? Now *you* are trying to move it back?"

Travis calmly looked at Hannibal. "How many boats have you guided off bars on this river?"

"I know how to spar a boat!"

"Doesn't matter – this happens all the time here. We've found those spars will support the boat even with the wheel turning backwards throwing water under the hull."

"Think you're smart don't you, driver?"

"You mean *pilot*, and if you weren't so busy brutalizing the crew you might get up this river easier than you–"

Before the words were out of Travis' mouth, Hannibal grabbed him by the throat with his right hand and began to squeeze.

Travis did his best to speak, "Pilot the boat yourself, you stupid ass...see how far you get."

Captain Hammermill heard their voices from his quarters and made his way to the pilothouse. He saw Hannibal's hand around Travis' throat and spoke in an uncharacteristically lucid voice, "Unhand him, Hannibal, or none of us will make it to West Port. I can promise you that."

Hannibal squeezed tighter then released Travis' throat. Travis coughed and spit on the floor of the pilothouse several times. Hannibal walked out saying, "I run this boat, old man."

After Hannibal was gone, Travis looked at Captain Hammermill and said in a raspy voice, "I don't know what's going on with you and Hannibal, but this is my last time on an HGM boat."

Captain Hammermill opened his bloodshot eyes wider. "Hell, young man – this could end up being everyone's last time on an HGM boat! Just get us to West Port."

As Hannibal descended the stairs, he felt the shudder of the bow hitting the sandbar again. The crew had moved the boat another few yards. When he reached the men at the capstan, he saw they were repeating the process and getting better at it. He looked over the starboard side and saw the paddle wheel moving water under and around the hull. There was easily three inches of water now under the boat which made the process that much easier. Travis saw Hannibal look over the side and quickly glance up at the pilothouse. Travis smiled. Hannibal frowned and walked away.

Harvey walked onto the main deck and called out, "Oh Hannibal – may I speak with you for a second?" Then he motioned to Hannibal with his right hand. Hannibal walked to the staircase and saw that Harvey had climbed the stairs to an area between floors out of sight from the main deck. Hannibal smiled. "You've been sleeping at your desk I see?"

"No...why?"

"There's a red button indentation on your forehead from the cuff of your shirt."

Harvey touched his forehead and sighed. "Never mind that. We're going to lose our opportunity if you keep running over those men."

"I'm the one that has to make *all this* happen!"

"The way you are doing it...is going to cost us."

"What?"

"You heard me. Keep this up and those passengers won't trust you to pour horse piss out of a boot."

"Nothing happens without *me* getting this done! We won't even get to West Port."

"Our goal is not West Port, you fool."

Hannibal stood silently in front of Harvey for a few seconds. "Okay what should we do?

"You must gain their trust. Getting off the bar cannot interfere with that."

"Physically scraping a steamboat over this much sand is never going to be *nice*, you little dilettante – what do you want me to do?"

"Change the dynamics. Sit the guy with the bleeding knee and take his place – get more crewmen to turn that thing on the deck and stop hitting people."

"Mr. Nice Guy."

"Call it what you like. Just do more. Pitch in – move the boat – be the hero, and save the day."

Hannibal stared at Harvey and sighed. "You might actually have something there, you little twit." Then he walked down the stairs and summoned more crew members to follow him. When he reached the bow, he stood over the crewman he hit with the log – bent down to his ear and whispered, "Let me push for a while."

The crewman said, "I can do it."

"I know you can. I *want* to help. Take a break – then come back and spell someone else."

The injured crewman stood up and Hannibal patted him on the back as he walked away – then bent down to push the capstan with the others.

On the shoreline, Gretchen stood up and pointed. "Did you see that? What came over him?"

Will said, "Perhaps he has a heart after all."

"I never would've believed it unless I saw it for myself," Clyde said. "He's doing the work now – look!"

Hannibal immediately set the pace working with the crew at the bow and moved the boat over the sandbar. Because of the constant use of the same muscles, however, their hands and legs cramped. Hannibal told the men at the capstan to take a break and ordered the rest of the crew to bring them food and water at the bow.

Following the break, the injured crewman Hannibal had beaten, saw they were getting closer to the water on the other side of the sandbar. He approached Hannibal and pleaded, "Let me finish this sir."

Hannibal stood and looked down at the young man whose knee stopped bleeding. He extended his hand and graciously replied, "She's all yours." The crewman shook Hannibal's hand and said, "I will get it done, sir."

Gretchen saw what was happening and yelled to everyone around her from George Town "Get off your butts, people! They're coming together. Let's encourage them."

Clyde yelled, "Come on! You're almost there!"

More passengers started yelling, "Go! Go! Go!" while

clapping their hands.

Hannibal joined in too, as the crewmen turned the capstan the last few feet. The crewmen repositioned the spars again, and Travis shouted into the tube, "Mr. Seagraves, one more time ought to do it!" The paddle wheel spun, and the bow rose one final time between the spars.

Travis was the first to notice something happening to the block attached to the larboard side spar. He shouted down to the crewmen at the bow. "Tackles' giving way! Look out!"

No crewman heard the warning because of all the cheers coming from the passengers on the riverbank and the rest of the crew.

Hannibal saw what was happening a split second later and shouted, "Look out!" and pointed at the spar, but it was too late. The top block broke free and struck a crewman in the back of the head. The larboard side of the boat immediately listed downward and the bow was forced left against the, now free, larboard side spar which fell outwards onto the sand. A split second later the starboard side spar followed the bow because it was still attached to it. Several crewmen scrambled to get out of the way, but it knocked two men down before landing hard and breaking one of the bars attached to the capstan.

Hannibal, himself, lifted the starboard spar a few inches to free a crewman who was trapped. Two other crewmen quickly helped him and pushed the spar over the bow onto the sand.

Hannibal looked at everyone attending to the crewman who was hit in the head. One turned to Hannibal with a somber stare and slowly shook his head. Hannibal looked closer and saw a bloody pants leg. He stared at the body of the crewman he had beaten, then looked back and saw Captain Hammermill walking toward him from the stairs with Harvey close behind. Because of the prolonged silence following the accident, those that didn't know exactly what had happened presumed there had been a death.

The captain told Hannibal, "Nothing you could have done, *son*. These boats have their dangers and I have seen them – far too often..."

Hannibal ignored him and went down to one knee beside the deceased crewman. When he knew everyone was watching, Hannibal publicly cried. "If only I had gotten there quicker..."

Captain Hammermill dutifully stood beside his first mate, placed his hand on Hannibal's back and solemnly proclaimed, "He's going to need a proper burial."

Harvey heard the words *proper burial* and walked back to the staircase. When Hannibal was finished talking to Captain Hammermill, he saw Harvey motioning at him. Hannibal briefly looked back at everyone at the bow and walked to the staircase. Harvey was not there, so he climbed the stairs to Harvey's office. After two light knocks, Hannibal opened the door – ducked his head and went in. Harvey was standing at the front of his desk – leaning over it arranging papers. Hannibal neglected to shut the door and tried to get past Harvey to sit in the chair. Harvey, at the same time, tried to get past Hannibal to quickly shut the door. Hannibal didn't like the fact that they were both occupying the same space, so he put both hands on Harvey's waist and forcefully attempted to move him toward the door. Then Hannibal's left knee hit the small chair and he lost his balance. He grabbed the back of Harvey's pants and pulled hard to steady himself. Harvey, however, was still holding the door knob. The opaque glass shattered when the door slammed shut and the chair made a loud cracking sound under Hannibal's weight.

Hannibal was now lying on chair pieces with Harvey on top of him. "God damn it! You little idiot! What the hell were you doing?"

"Trying to shut the door before anyone sees us together."

"They're all on shore, you little sprite! Now get off me before the rest of the crew thinks there's been another accident and comes running up here!"

Harvey used the desk to steady himself and stood saying, "You're absolutely right. Let's go to the hurricane deck." After stating his intention, Harvey promptly walked out of his office – closing the door and leaving Hannibal lying on the deck with pieces of the chair and glass scattered over the floor.

Hannibal was not surprised to hear the footsteps of someone running up the stairs. He sat up and saw his second mate through the broken glass.

"You alright sir?" said the man Hannibal had lifted over his head and thrown into the Mississippi River in St. Louis.

"Yes, everything's fine. I...tripped."

Jason Winship looked through the broken glass at Hannibal sitting on the remains of the chair and said, "As you say, sir. We're preparing the body."

"Thank you. Gather his effects. I will be there in a few minutes."

"Aye, sir – are you sure you don't need any–"

Hannibal raised his right hand, as if to signal a halt to the conversation. Then one of the remaining shards of glass at the top of the door frame dropped and bounced off the lower part of the frame before landing on the floor with a *plink* as it hit another piece of glass. Jason's eyes briefly met Hannibal's. He felt himself beginning to convulse, but quickly covered his laughter with a pretend cough and walked back down the stairs.

Hannibal got to his feet, brushed off little pieces of glass, and went to the hurricane deck. He saw Harvey looking out past the paddle wheel at the stern. They both saw a flat shallow trench the width of the boat that extended fifty yards to the water on the other side. Large holes were in the sand on the sides of the trench where the spars had been placed. Hannibal stood close to Harvey, gently placed his hands on the rail and inquired, "What was so important back there that made you feel the need to destroy your office?"

"You were the one that grabbed me! I was trying to shut the door to keep our conversation secret."

"Secret! A man just died. The boat was completely silent. *Everyone* heard what just happened."

"I think you're exaggerating."

"What? The passengers all the way out on that riverbank heard the chair breaking under my ass, you dimwitted little–"

"Hannibal–"

"Harvey – even the last of the Indians out here probably heard you break that glass."

"Hannibal, we can *use* the burial of that crewman."

"What?"

"Have a talk with Richards. Apologize to him for your actions and the tragedy. Tell him you need to dig a grave for the crewman on some higher ground or something like that – just so you're far enough away from the boat."

"But I would have to come back alone?"

"Like you just said. We blame it on the Indians. Isn't that what everyone else does out here?"

Hannibal stared out at the trench for a few moments.

"Harvey – I knew there was *some* reason Draggart got you as a front man for this. You really are a devious little shit aren't you?"

Harvey smiled.

CHAPTER SIXTEEN
DEAD RECKONING

O nce the *Empire Lander* was free of the sandbar, Travis piloted to the point on the north bank of the Missouri River where the passengers and their possessions were gathered for reloading.

Will had been helping passengers organize the largest items to the smallest. Once he saw the steamboat moving toward them, he said, "Okay, Miles – here it comes. We're finally ready to get going again."

"I know Will, but remember all these people and their children just saw a man die right before their eyes."

"I hear you, Miles. I'm not getting on anyone yet, but it's getting dark and these people are stronger than you think."

The *Empire Lander* moved slowly to the north river-bank. Harvey reached up and placed his hand on Hannibal's back as they looked at the passengers who were gathering to re-board and said, "Alright, Hannibal – let's see what you've got."

Hannibal walked out to the bow and helped the other crewmen with the gangplank. He then, ran ashore and tied a rope from the cavels at the bow to a tree. More crewmen came out the gangplank to help carry the passenger's trunks, but Hannibal held his hand up to them, and they stopped. Then he turned to face the passengers and raised his voice. "I am sorry for what happened here today, and I take full responsibility."

Miles leaned over to Will and whispered, "He's owning up to it."

Martin Clearman shouted, "Hannibal – no one is responsible for that tackle breaking. It was an accident!"

"Hannibal raised both arms and said, "No – they were following my orders – no one else's – the crew will now help all of you back on the boat."

The first person in line was Gretchen. Hannibal lifted her trunk over his head and walked up the gangplank. Other crew members grabbed trunks for passengers and brought them to their staterooms as fast as they could. Hannibal never stopped. He made trips up and down the gangplank and up the stairs to the staterooms on the boiler deck until everyone's belongings were back in place.

Once they were aboard, Will, Miles, Ian and Nate sat on their trunks together and drank after a late dinner. Ian, holding a whisky filled metal cup to his mouth said stoically said, "Will, the only thing good about that whole experience was that we have less muck and piss in here right now."

Nate smiled. "Ian, that might be the most intelligent thing you've said this entire trip."

Ian took a long sip from the cup and raised his right hairy eyebrow. "You coming at me, Nate?"

"No, Ian – I mean it. If I had known better, I would have gladly walked beside my wagon all the way from Kentucky rather than spend any amount of time in these wretched conditions."

Will shook his head. "Come on now, look at the bright side. We're shaving weeks off this trip taking these damned boats. You're going to get your share of walking, I promise. Think of Abigail and Caleb. They aren't down here smelling it or listening to you gripe."

"You're right, Will. I think I'll go up and see them again – like right now."

Ian heard something and looked toward the bow. "What was that?'

Miles said, "I think its Hannibal. I didn't recognize him at first because he's wearing a shirt."

"Will took another sip from his cup, then stood up and looked toward the bow. He seems to be moving, Miles, but I can't tell what he's doing from here."

"He's crying, Will."

"Hannibal doesn't cry."

"I guess he does."

Will gestured with his right hand and said, "Give me that bottle. I bet it's about that crewman." Then, Will walked to the bow and saw their first mate sobbing. "Hannibal, it's not your fault."

Hannibal rubbed his eyes with the sleeves of his shirt. "I don't know, Will. He was new – I should have checked the tackle on both those spars."

"Hannibal, you can only control so much."

Hannibal looked at Will with watery red eyes. "I beat that young man like crewmen beat *me* when I was his age. I'm as bad now as they were then."

"He knew this trip wasn't a cake walk, Hannibal. Don't people die on these rivers every day?"

Hannibal took out a handkerchief – blew his nose, and mournfully said, "Yes."

"Well, we haven't made it to West Port yet. Let's get busy and make sure he's the *only* one that dies on this trip."

Hannibal, slowly looked at up at Will with an empty stare, as if he was going to speak, but instead, shook his head and said nothing.

"No matter what happens right now, you can't bring

him back."

"You're right, Will."

Will gave Hannibal the whisky bottle and said, "It's been a long day, Hannibal. Calm down for a second and have a drink."

Hannibal took a sip, then handed the bottle back to Will and declared, "I must dig a grave for him at dawn."

"Where?"

"Up on that hill that was behind your group on the riverbank today."

"Why so far?"

"Floods on this river can wash everything away below the high ground. It's not going to happen to *his* grave."

"You're going to dig the entire grave by yourself?"

Hannibal looked in the direction of the hill behind them and piously answered, "Yes, I must to do this myself...and for the crew."

Will sighed. "Hannibal, I know how you feel and I don't care what you say – I'm going to help you. It'll be quicker that way."

"I didn't want this to be a big thing, Will. It's something I must do quietly...alone."

"Hannibal, I won't say a word. Dig in silence if you like, but *I'm* going to help you. Then we can put all this behind us and be on our way that much sooner."

Hannibal took a big swig and handed the bottle back to Will. "I leave at dawn."

"Great – see you then."

On his way to bed, Hannibal saw some of the crew preparing the boat for departure and said, "Jason."

Jason Winship stood. "Aye sir."

"Jason, I'm going out in the morning to dig the grave, and I insist on doing it alone."

"As you say, sir."

"One more thing – Will, for some reason, is asking to help me. If you or the rest of the crew see him coming to help, it's all right. You men continue to get the boat ready to leave."

"Very well, sir."

At the first light of day, Ian was awakened by a rushing sound coming from the southwest. He rose from the pallet behind his trunk and shouted, "Sandstorm!" Miles sat up as fast as he could to see what was happening and a large flurry of sand hit him in the face. He crouched back behind his trunk and yelled, "Ouch – damn it! Someone get me water for my eyes. I can't see!"

Ian placed his cup of water next to Miles. "Idiot! What's the first thing you *don't do* if someone yells *sandstorm!*"

Miles began feeling for the cup of water when a smattering of hail hit the boat. "Shut up, Ian, and get me some more water. This hurts."

Will opened his eyes. "What the hell is going on!"

Nate, still on the pallet behind his trunk interjected, "Fire and brimstone, Will – stay down, and you won't end up crawling around like Miles over there trying to find water with his eyes shut."

"I can't – I've got to get up and help Hannibal dig that poor crewmen's grave."

From behind his trunk, Ian remarked, "That's the stupidest thing I've ever heard. Let him dig his own grave. He's the one that got that boy killed."

"Come on, Ian – you know it's not his fault the tackle came off that spar. He feels horrible about it. I told him I'd help. He's doing it for the crew."

"Suit yourself, Will. I thought Miles was the biggest idiot so far today until you opened *your* mouth. You and the goon have fun digging a grave in the sandstorm."

Will stood up – tied a handkerchief around his face and

grabbed a shovel. "Shut up, Ian – have a little compassion!" Then he walked to the bow and saw the vague image of Hannibal carrying a pickaxe and shovel up the hill. Then he went back to Nate. "Didn't we bring a pickaxe too?"

"Yep – it's in the corner by Dominick."

Will walked out the gangplank with the shovel and pickaxe and began a light jog up the hill to catch Hannibal. He thought, *At least the wind and sand are at my back now.* Once he was within sixty yards, he shouted, "Hannibal, slow up!"

Hannibal shielded his eyes from the sand and enthusiastically replied, "Will – good morning!"

"Who ordered all this wind and the sand?"

Hannibal laughed. "Not me."

Will ran up to him shouting, "We'll get this done, Hannibal." When he was only a few yards away, he said, "Where do you go after this?"

"Will, you really didn't have to. After this, I'm sure we'll pick up freight and pas-sengers back to St. Louis – guess you're looking at land out west?"

"You know it. Have you ever thought about the West?"

Hannibal glanced behind him. He saw Will trying to keep up. "No, Will – my home is on these rivers."

Will found himself breathing much heavier and asked, "How much further do you want to go?"

"Over the ridge by that big willow tree. It will be a marker for his relatives. We owe him that much."

"They'll find it with no problem," Will said. "All we have to do is tell them it's the big hill to the north after the giant bar."

As they crested the ridge and approached the tree, Hannibal somberly proclaimed, "I think this will do."

"Yeah, and we're shielded from that wind and dust

now too."

"Will – I'll break up the soil with the pick first, and you shovel out behind me."

"Okay, I'll leave my pick over here."

Hannibal pulled his pickaxe along the ground forming the outline of a large rectangle.

"He's not that big, Hannibal."

"The sides always tend to narrow as we dig. It will be fine."

"Okay, Hannibal – have at it."

Hannibal swung the pickaxe over his head and broke the top soil very quickly. He worked with Will right behind him, shoveling dirt to one side of the grave. After a few more minutes. Will stopped to wipe sweat from his face. "You're making quick work of this. You also flip to the axe quickly for those tree roots. It looks like you've dug graves before."

Hannibal's eyebrows rose. He briefly stopped swinging the pickaxe, but never turned to face Will. Then he swung it back over his head and meekly said, "Not really – just ditches some time ago."

Back on the *Empire Lander*, Ian noticed that no one was serving breakfast. He raised his voice over the wind. "Nate, do we not get to eat today?"

Nate, still lying behind his trunk, said, "Maybe it's the storm, Ian – give the crew a break."

"They can break in West Port. I'm hungry now!"

"Well, Ian – why don't you go upstairs and tell the captain yourself?"

Miles, still lying on his pallet said, "Yeah, Ian – go up there and give the captain a piece of your mind!"

Ian walked toward the stairs covering his eyes with a handkerchief. "It's not just about my belly – I'm thinking of the women and children upstairs with no food, too."

Nate sat up with a closed eye to the wind. "Come on, Ian – you know it's all about your belly."

Ian pulled his hat down over his face. "I still can't believe I've let myself become subjected to this fool hardy trip – doing nothing while we're on shore and wallowing in horse shit with no food while we're on the boat. I'll be taking the next boat back to St. Louis!"

Nate stood, shielding his eyes with his shirtsleeve. "Do all the Scots become eccentric whiners like you?"

Ian yelled, "Do all the builders sit on their asses and bark orders like you – or do you actually work some too?"

Nate, briefly lost his dignity and shouted, "Go blow it out your bagpipe – you, pestilent old man!"

Miles quickly said, "He got you down to his level pretty quick that time, Nate – you're wasting your breath. Now please get me more water to flush my eyes."

When Ian reached the hurricane deck, he saw no one, so he knocked on the captain's door and waited. There wasn't a response, so he decided to go in. When the door opened, the daylight caught the frail image of Captain Hammermill passed out on his bed, and dressed only in an old white T-shirt and his uniform pants. Next to him, on the desk, was a near empty bottle of whisky. Also on the desk were various papers. Some were freight lists, but what caught Ian's eye was a letter to Captain Hammermill, typed under the engraved letterhead of *Horace, Greeley & Montgomery*. The letter was addressed to a post office box in St. Louis. Among other things, the letter discussed payment arrangements for the crew's trip to West Port and was signed by Riley Draggart, as accountant for the company.

Ian thought of the letters *HGM* proudly welded to the spacer bar between the smokestacks and looked back at the unconscious captain. Then he suddenly had a strong feeling that something terrible was about to happen. He left the captain's quarters and ran down the stairwell holding the rails and running his hands against the walls so he wouldn't fall.

Harvey, sporting a well tailored jacket now because of the weather, heard someone clamoring down the steps outside of his office and poked his head out the door to see what was happening.

Nate heard Ian rounding the staircase on the main deck. "What do you want now, old man?"

"There was a letter up there! Greeley owns this boat! I think Will's in trouble – the goon's with him right now!"

Nate grabbed his powder horn and rifle.

Ian walked a few steps toward the bow and pointed emphatically at the hill and exclaimed, "Nate, there's no time to load a gun or saddle a horse. You're the only one on this boat that can get to that ridge fast enough – now go!"

Nate ran back to Dominick and grabbed his saddlebag full of small hatchets and knives. Then he hurried to the bow shielding his eyes from the sand.

Ian stopped right before the bow; and as Nate hurried by, he quietly said, "Try not to alert those crewmen over there."

"How am I *not* going to do that, old man? I'm walking right by them."

"We don't know who's involved in all this."

"We are getting ready to find out." Then, Nate walked past the crew members bringing wood aboard, tipped his hat and said, "Going to help." The crewmen continued working and never looked up. When Nate reached the riverbank, he sprinted up the hill.

Harvey was halfway up the stairwell and out of sight from the main deck. He saw Nate walk past the crew members and bolt up the hill, so he wasted no time in getting down to them and asked, "Where did he say he was going?"

One of the men stacking wood with a hand over his eyes said, "He's going to help with something." Harvey peered through small gaps between his fingers in order to see and ran as fast as he could behind Nate.

Miles, still lying behind his trunk, heard footsteps coming from the bow. "Ian, is that you?

"Yes."

"What was all the rushing around and footsteps, and why were you whispering to Nate?"

Ian kneeled down to Miles and whispered in his ear. Miles sat up and tried to open his eyes. "I've got to go, too."

Ian saw Mile's lower eye lids still contained sand. Tears were flowing down his cheeks from the irritation. "You're useless, Miles – you're not going anywhere. You can't even see!"

"I've got to do something!"

"Then go stumble around – make a scene and try to get medical help at the bow – just keep the crew occupied while I get to the top of this boat with my guns."

"Stumble around at the bow?"

"Should be easy for you now. Besides, it'll be a good sign if they help you."

"But what if they don't help?"

"Then they're probably with the ones trying to kill Will."

"Shit – why do these things only happen when I'm stuck with you?"

"Stop your blathering and get out there, because right now I'm going to visit our two-faced captain and find some things out...the hard way."

As Nate ran up the hill, the sunrise caught the light brown color of the sand in the air. Strong gusts continued to rip through the river valley bending branches and throwing all manner of debris into the air.

Nate heard a high voice behind him shouting, "Hannibal! Hannibal!" so, he decided to duck behind a tree where the makeshift path narrowed. He poked his head out slightly to see it was Harvey. The tree shielded him from another large gust of sand; but, Nate was able to see Harvey running with one hand over his face, and the other in his stylish jacket and wondered, *What's in the other hand?* Harvey's footsteps became louder as he ran, and when he was almost even with the tree, he screamed, "Hannibal watch out for the–" But before he could finish his warning, the full weight of the saddle bag hit him in the teeth. Harvey was completely upended and landed on the back of his head. The flap of the saddle bag broke loose from the impact. Knives and hatchets were thrown from the bag and scattered over several yards.

Nate leaned over Harvey and said, "Watch out for the what? little man." Then, he grabbed a hatchet by Harvey's head and continued running up the hill.

The strong winds carrying sand finally died down. Jason Winship and the crew had just finished attaching a new block and tackle to the spars when they heard someone stumble and fall onto the deck by the bow. "Help – I can't see," cried Miles.

Jason quickly looked around, saw Miles on the deck and said, "The man needs help – come on!"

Two other crewmen kneeled to Miles and asked, "What happened to you?"

Miles writhed on the deck in pain screaming, "My eyes!"

Another crewman came to the bow. "Lay still – let me

see."

Ian quietly walked up the stairs to the hurricane deck carrying a pistol and a rifle and saw the crew members below attending to Miles. With his face up, one of the young crewmen pulled down on Miles' cheek under his right eye and, at the same time, pulled his upper right eyelid into his right eyebrow. Then, another crewman flushed Miles' eye with water.

Hannibal sighed. "All right, Will – you break it up for a while. I'm getting some water." Hannibal took a few steps back and watched Will take the pickaxe he was using. He swung it several times overhead and tore up the ground as fast as he could. Hannibal saw Will's focus was on getting the job done quickly because he never looked behind himself. Hannibal then, slowly and quietly, took a few steps back and picked up the other shovel. Will pulled the pickaxe back over his head again, but this time he saw the rapidly moving shadow of a long strait object coming toward him. He instinctively jumped left and the head of the shovel hit the ground next to him with a *PLUNK*."

Will rolled left – looked back at Hannibal and shouted, "What in the hell are you doing!"

Hannibal raised the shovel and swung it as fast and hard as he could. Will, now on his back, quickly rolled right this time. The shovel hit the ground again and missed his head by inches. Will reached to grab the shaft of the shovel, but Hannibal pulled it back too quickly. Hannibal coolly said, "It's no use Will – I'm sorry."

Will knew he had to get up, but Hannibal was too fast, so he watched and decided to time his roll so he could be closer to the shovel when it hit the ground. Hannibal swung it again. Will rolled, but this time he reached out and quickly got a hand on the shaft. Hannibal tried to pull it back but couldn't. With his free hand, Will grabbed dirt and threw it in Hannibal's face. Hannibal, still clutching the shovel with his right hand, moved backwards to rub his eyes. Will jumped to his feet. Hannibal took a step toward him and swung the shovel sideways, but Will blocked the shaft with his left arm. Then, he lunged and hit Hannibal in the jaw. Hannibal was unfazed and grabbed the shaft of the shovel with two hands spaced apart – then pushed Will flat onto the side of the unfinished grave. Will squirmed because the shaft was across his throat now and he couldn't breathe. He violently tried to dig his heels into the ground to push himself away, but his feet slipped one after another until he stopped moving.

Hannibal never heard the footsteps behind him. Nate saw the pickaxe that Will had leaned against the tree. He dropped the hatchet, grabbed the handle of the pickaxe with both hands and swung it behind his head, then fell to his left knee as he threw it over his head. The pickaxe rotated once over a distance of fifteen feet and hit Hannibal hard in the middle of his back with a *THUMP.* The impact threw Hannibal onto Will's body. He frantically reached back to touch whatever hit him. After a few more seconds of desperately reaching for the pickaxe, his body lost life.

Nate jumped into the shallow unfinished grave and shouted, "Will – you still alive?" Neither of the bodies moved. Nate pulled Hannibal's body away, then he felt Will's chest to see if he was breathing.

Will, with his eyes still shut, coughed and said in a raspy whisper. "I'm not your wife, Nate."

Nate's leaned back and started taking in deep breaths. "You're half-dead and you're still a smart-ass! I thought we lost you, big man."

Will gently felt his throat. "I don't know what happen-ed. We were digging this grave, and he started swinging that shovel at me."

"All I know is Ian was looking for food and went to the captain's quarters. Then he came down the stairs faster than I've ever seen him move. He told me that Greeley owns the boat and you were in trouble. I ran out here as quick as I could. I think the clerk was in on it too."

"That little guy with the tight clothes?"

"Yeah *him.* He was running behind me shouting Hannibal's name. I thought he had a gun, so I wanted to knock him down, but I think I hit him too hard."

"Anyone else? What about the captain?"

"Maybe, because of what Ian found. I don't know who else – but I do know this – if it weren't for Ian's stomach – you'd be dead right now."

"Greeley?"

"Yes Greeley."

"We were already gone – what did he care?"

"I know – It doesn't make any sense, but what do we do now?"

"With Greeley?"

"No – The little man and Hannibal."

Will slowly stood up. "We have to get to the pilot and that second mate. Winship was his name, I think."

Nate frowned. "What if they were in on it as well and we can't get back on the boat?"

Will thought for a second. "Ian was right – I'm a complete idiot, but Hannibal wanted me alone for a reason, so maybe the rest of the crew isn't part of it."

"The crewmen I passed didn't seem to care when I ran up here."

Will ran his fingers through his hair, and after a few seconds said, "Maybe Hannibal's *act* was just for the rest of the crew?"

Nate looked at Hannibal's body lying a few feet away with a large amount of blood pooling around him and stated, "No matter who was part of this, what are we going to say about the bodies?"

"The rest of the crew couldn't be part of Greeley's plan otherwise I'd be dead."

"So we walk back and say Hannibal tried to murder you?"

"Not yet – because if other crewmen are still involved they might say we murdered Hannibal and his little friend. The rest of the crew might believe it."

"Then what gets us back on the boat, Will?"

Will thought for a moment. "Indians."

"We blame it on Indians?

"At least for now – because the good crewman might believe it, and that gets us on the boat too without being put in chains first."

"You may be overthinking it Will. Besides aren't most of the Indians gone now after the Relocation Act?"

"Damn it Nate! I don't know what to think right now – I literally still have one foot in this grave."

"Yeah, but the Indians – really?"

"It's all we've got. We didn't cause this mess. Do you have a better idea?"

"No."

"Okay then – see if anyone's coming up here yet."

Nate ran down the ridge to see if anyone from the boat was coming toward them. Will slowly walked over to the top of the ridge to get a better view. Nate shouted, "There's no one, Will."

"Okay, let's see what we've got with that agent." When they reached Harvey's body, Will said, "Good god Nate – did you *ever* put the hit on him!" It was obvious that

Harvey's jaw had been broken, and he bled heavily from his mouth and the back of his head before he died.

"Like I said Will, I didn't think he made it. What do we do?"

"Damn Nate – do you think you brought enough hatchets and knives?"

"Ian kept hurrying me! I didn't know who was out here. I just grabbed the bag and ran."

"Tell you what – let's gather up all your toys, and go lose them over there in those trees."

"Okay Will, but what do we do with the bodies?"

"Nothing."

"We leave them the way they are?"

"You bet we do – we've just lived through a bad Indian attack where Hannibal and his little friend were killed, remember?"

Ian proceeded into Captain Hammermill's quarters without knocking. The captain was sitting up on his bed now, but still wearing the same shabby undershirt and uniform pants. His shoes and socks were a few feet away from him on the floor. Ian said, "Hello, did you have a good nap?"

The captain shouted, "Who the hell are you?"

Ian closed the door and said, "Sorry Captain – I'm asking the questions today." After placing his pistol on the captain's desk, he propped his rifle by the door. Then, he picked up one of the socks on the floor and walked toward the captain. The captain's eyebrows rose and his eyes widened before he demanded, "What the hell are you–"

Before he could finish, Ian shoved the sock in the captain's mouth, then pulled him off the bed and dragged him to his desk chair. The captain made severable indiscernible sounds before Ian forced his left hand to the desk and grabbed the white hair on the back of his head. Then he turned the captain's head, and bent it down six inches from a piece of paper on the desk. "See this letter here from Riley Draggart? You are going to let me know who else, besides yourself, is in on Mr. Greeley's little game." Then Ian pulled the sock out of the captain's mouth.

He gasped for air and attempted to say, "I am the captain of this boat and you–"

Ian quickly shoved the sock back in the captain's mouth and looked at corner of the desk. "Apparently you're not listening – but hey! Look at this! Someone didn't get their butter knife and saucer back to the galley." Ian picked up the butter knife with a strong grip and placed the dull blade on the little finger of the captain's left hand. The captain's eyes widened before Ian firmly pressed the butter knife through the finger." The captain let out a muffled, "AAAGH." Tears rolled down his face. A few seconds past before he put his head on the desk and tapped Ian three times with his right hand.

"Are you ready to tell me what I want to know?"

With his head still lying on the desk, the captain nodded.

Ian pulled the sock out of the captain's mouth. "Good – here, use this sock to stem the bleeding. There's another on the floor if we need it – now who else is involved?"

The captain sat up and his uncut white hair fell forward. Then, he wrapped the sock around his bleeding finger and stated, "Greeley will kill me."

Ian, who was still behind the captain, leaned over him and softly said, "I'm the one that's here and ready to take the thumb now – not Greeley – so have a drink and tell me what I want to know." Then Ian poured the remainder of the whisky from the bottle into a glass next to the captain.

The captain sighed, and pushed his hair back over his head before he took a large sip – then placed the glass on the desk. "Hannibal and the clerk."

"That's it? Just you – the goon and the midge? You're kidding?"

Suddenly, they heard shouting from the main deck. Ian picked up his pistol from the desk and said in a low voice. "Stand up – we're going to the railing. As they walked from the captain's quarters, Ian placed the barrel of the pistol against the captain's back.

One of the crewmen on the main deck shouted to Jason Winship, "Something's happened – it looks like someone's injured!"

Jason made his way to the bow from the stern shouting as he walked, "Is it Hannibal?"

"No, that tall passenger – he's limping. His friend that ran out there late is helping him."

"Where's Hannibal?"

Another crewman shouted, "I don't see him – only the two passengers."

Sarah, Gretchen and Abigail came out of their rooms and gathered at the railing on the starboard sides of the main and boiler decks. Abigail saw Nate helping Will to the boat and yelled "Nathaniel, what are you doing out there?"

Ian, still high above everyone else on the hurricane deck, poked the captain in the back with his pistol and softly said, "Saints be praised, Captain, you may live through this after all. When Will and Nate get close enough to hear you, order them to your quarters." Ian poked the captain with his pistol again and whispered, "Got it?"

The captain swallowed. "Yes, I've got it."

Travis, who had been sleeping, came out of his quarters. "Captain what is it?"

Ian moved the pistol under his coat and answered Travis. "We don't really know quite yet. They were digging the grave this morning and some are coming back. Right Captain?"

"Uh...yes – we will see what happens here – I'll let you know."

Travis looked at Ian. "You're with the Richards party. I met Will earlier in the trip. I'm Travis Wheeler." Then Travis extended his right hand.

Ian's eyes focused on the extended hand. Since his pistol was in his right hand, he reached out with his left and explained, "Got to shake with me left today, Travis. I twisted the right arm messing with the horses."

Travis glanced at Ian's right arm under his coat. "That's okay – Captain, are you all right?"

"Yes – never better."

Travis looked down and saw the sock stretched around the captain's left hand. "What happened to your left hand, Captain?"

Jason saw Will limping and holding onto Nate. He shouted as loud as he could, "Will – what happened?"

Will yelled back, "Indians! – over the ridge – it was horrible – they killed Hannibal!"

Gretchen, Elizabeth and Abigail, in unison, said "Indians!" and began to gather children back into the staterooms.

Jason looked up toward the ridge, then glanced back at Nate and Will and shouted, "Arm yourselves men! Everyone stay on the boat. That's an order." Crew members scrambled for the boat's rifles and ammo. As each crewman grabbed a rifle and loaded it, they took a position at the starboard side railing. After that, one by one, every passenger that brought a gun on board began to find wherever they had placed their powder and loaded their rifles.

Will and Nate reached the gangplank and Captain Hammermill shouted, "Will, you and your friend come up here at once! That's an order!"

Will whispered to Nate, "I don't know about that."

Nate looked up and saw Ian and Travis with the Captain. "It's okay – Ian's there."

Jason shouted to the Captain, "Do you need me too, sir?"

"No! If Hannibal *is* dead, you're the first mate now. You men protect the boat while I talk to them!"

"Aye Captain!"

Will and Nate made their way up the stairs. When Will saw Miles, he said simply, "Your eyes?"

"I'm okay, Will – but you look like shit."

Will winked at Miles. "Thanks – I'll fill you in later."

Miles saw Nate was smiling as they went up the stairs, but wasn't sure what was going on, so he went back to the horses.

When Will and Nate reached the hurricane deck, Captain Hammermill said, "Come in here gentlemen. We need to talk."

Since Travis never received an answer, he repeated himself. "Captain, what about your hand?"

"The hand's fine. Fortunately, God blessed me with two. See what needs to be done to get the ship ready to go while I visit with these men."

Travis looked unsure at Captain Hammermill and muttered, "Aye sir," and walked back to the pilothouse.

Ian opened the captain's door. "Come in, let's have a little visit."

When they walked in, Ian held his pistol outside his coat. Will smiled, "Captain, I can see that you've met Ian."

Ian motioned to the captain to sit behind his desk, then picked up the letter from Riley Draggart and handed it to Will. "Our good captain has something to say."

Will looked at the letter then looked up at Captain Hammermill. "That big son of a bitch tried to kill me out there."

The captain silently stared at Will with the expression of a child caught misbehaving. Ian broke the moment. "He told me that Greeley got the captain here, Hannibal, and the little agent to kill you."

Will took his hat off and threw it at Captain Hammermill. "Greeley bought a steamboat line just to kill *me* hundreds of miles from Kentucky?"

Nate laughed. "I guess he thought that was the best way to get away with it."

Will stared at Captain Hammermill for a few moments. "You worthless old drunk – you're really not that good at anything are you?"

Captain Hammermill slouched further into his chair. He began to answer, but Will cut him off.

"It's ironic – you may be the only one of your sophomoric friends to live through this."

"I only attended to the paperwork," muttered the Captain.

"You're as guilty as Hannibal and that little gnat of his, but none of us wants to wait around for the trial of an incompetent old drunk. We're getting out west as soon as we can."

Captain Hammermill smiled. "I'm happy to oblige."

"Of course you are – you, sorry old piece of shit! Let me tell you now – this is what's going to happen. You're going to get out there and tell the crew the silly Indian story – then we go on about our way to West Port and never see you or this river valley again."

"What about that young man that was killed at the bow?"

"Tell the crew it's too dangerous here – then get up river and bury him someplace closer to the boat."

Captain Hammermill stood and smiled. "So that's it then?"

"No – you're telling the crew Ian and you have become such good friends that he's welcome in your cabin anytime."

Ian left his post at the door and walked behind the captain – put his arm around him and boomed, "Good idea, Will – just keep the whisky and the food coming! I'll see to it that the captain here lives up to our low expectations of him."

Captain Hammermill sat back down at his desk and buried his face into his hands again.

As Will and Nate were walking out the door, Ian said, "We'll do a good job running this boat together – I can help with the burial too."

Captain Hammermill raised his head. "The burial?"
"Sure Captain – how's about starting off with this? Yeah, though I walk through the *river* valley of the shadow of death..."

CHAPTER SEVENTEEN
MIXED BLESSING

Will made his way to the captain's quarters again. Ian and Captain Hammermill were finishing another breakfast. Playing cards were scattered over the desk along with two empty whisky bottles. The captain said, "Let me tell you what happened with the boiler explosion. It was about three years ago when I told them..."

Ian used his napkin to wipe his mouth, then turned to Will and rolled his eyes. "I know – I know – the boiler exploded because they didn't do what you said. It's the third time I've heard the story in two days! I think I've got it, Chet. Will, we need more coffee."

"I see you two are on a first-name basis now."

Ian threw his napkin down. "No amount of food and whisky is worth this. I've had it. Get me off this boat."

"I was thinking of asking the good captain to come with us so you could continue your conversation across North America."

Ian shut his eyes. "Okay, Will – you got me – we're even."

Will looked at the mess Ian and the captain created. He laughed out loud as he walked out the door embellishing Ian's defeat by raising his right fist.

Ian shouted at him as he walked away, "You'd be in a shallow grave right now if it wasn't for me, Will Richards!"

At the pilothouse, Will saw Travis standing at the wheel gently moving it one way – then the other and always being careful not to over steer. "Good morning, Travis. What do you think?"

"A while longer – river level's good here. We'll be passing Lexington soon, then Independence and the West Port Landing."

"Great, Travis. Funny coming all this way from one Lexington to another."

"Okay, Will – whatever. Since you and your men control this boat now, you're not going to tell me what really happened back there are you?"

"At the funeral for that young man?"

"That ridiculous ceremony?"

"I've seen better Travis."

"Will, the crewmen ran out and took rifle positions at miles of *nothing*. Then we had two quick bible verses from a captain that can't remember his own name."

Will grinned. "Okay – what do you think really happened back there with Hannibal and the agent?"

"They got killed, but it wasn't by your *pretend* Indians."

"Look Travis, we didn't know who else was in on it. Besides, if you knew something was going on, why didn't you say something?" Then, Will turned and had almost walked out of the pilothouse before Travis raised his voice.

"There's lots of no good people, like Hannibal, that work these rivers every day without trying to kill someone!"

Will looked back from the doorway. "We aren't waiting around West Port for the wheels of justice to deal with that old drunk. My advice to you is take his ass back to St. Louis and walk away."

Travis looked forward at the river for a few seconds. "What's he supposed to do in St. Louis after all this?"

"I don't know. Who cares? He's trash. But one thing I *do* know – he won't stick around to face the bastard from Kentucky that's been after me."

"I understand, Will. We'll put him in his quarters – keep him liquored up and humor him. He won't be a problem. I'm sorry about the trip. I'm glad that big sneaky son of a bitch is dead, but I had no idea he was trying to kill anyone."

Will pointed at Travis. "It might not be *your* fault, but I'm not happy with anything that's happened on this sorry trip other than arriving in one piece and getting on dry land! Captain Bridges was right about Hannibal, and I didn't listen." Then, Will left the pilothouse, walked down the stairs, and saw that this would probably be the last boat trip Joseph would ever take with Katherine and Elizabeth.

"Will, there you are. All I've been hearing for the past hour is, *how much longer do we have, Daddy?*"

"Tell them to pack up, Joseph – another hour or so."

"Thank God. We're sick of this boat."

"Well, good. You'll have about six months to stretch your legs now."

"Sorry, Will. I know you've been through a lot."

"No, it's all right. We're still trying to figure out what happened back there."

"Here or on the Ohio?"

"Ha! The guys on the Ohio were from generations of idiots. We had a lot more here on this boat."

"Greeley?"

"Think so."

"We have to do something then."

"I don't know, Joseph. The further west we go – the

less it'll matter."

"Will, If Greeley came after you this far away from Kentucky, what makes you think you're safe now?"

"Come on Joseph – who's he going to buy this far west?"

"Might be easier for him out here. There's less law the farther west we go."

"Joseph, let's worry about getting our wagons put back together as soon as we dock. I need to go down and help with the horses right now."

"Alright but what about–"

Joseph was interrupted by Sammy McConnell running around the deck screaming "We're almost there! We're almost there!" Katherine Hinrichs heard Sammy and ran out of her room after him.

Caleb heard the other children and ran out of his stateroom door. Abigail shouted, "Not another step young man!" Caleb froze and did not make another move.

Clyde McConnell ran up the stairs yelling "Slow down!" No one's going to get hurt right before we even get there!"

Gretchen poked her head out of her doorway. "Clyde, these kids have been cooped up for too long. They need to run!"

"Gretchen, we've come this far without losing a child. Let's keep it that way! They're going to get all the exercise they want after we get off this boat."

Katherine lengthened her stride and passed Sammy on the railing as she ran around the deck. They were both running toward Joseph who extended his arms to keep them from falling. "Whoa now, children! Slow down before you fall off the boat."

Katherine stood and pointed to the south river bank. Joseph saw that she was looking at a steamboat tied to a dock. Past the dock were a series of very steep bluffs that lined the river. "Is that it? Are we here?"

Clyde walked closer to her. "No sweetheart, I think that's Independence."

"That's all there is, Mr. McConnell?"

"The town is way back over those steep hills, Katherine. It's much bigger. What you see there is Blue Mills landing. There's another landing coming up too before ours. It's called Wayne City."

As the *Empire Lander* passed the landing, Katherine asked, "Why didn't we stop there Mr. McConnell?"

"We wanted to get a little farther west so we didn't have to cross a river that's coming up."

"What river?"

"The Big Blue River."

"Why do they call it blue?"

Joseph smiled. "You'll be here all day with this one, Clyde."

"It's okay – all those questions show how smart she is."

Katherine now was doing her best to keep Joseph between her and Sammy because he kept trying to grab her arm. Joseph pulled them both in front of him. "They're *really* ready to get off this boat."

"I think we all are, Joseph. It's not been pleasant down there in the horse manure."

Later, on the main deck, Miles was quietly enjoying a cup of coffee at the bow. He realized this part of their trip was over and walked back to Will and the horses.

Will asked, "We there yet?"

"I think we're about done. We've past the other landings. West Port is next."

"Yes! Thank God. Hopefully before Ian strangles the captain. The old fart won't shut up."

"You sticking Ian with that guy was brilliant – best

thing you've done the whole trip."

Will continued shoveling the area around Lucky. "Yeah Miles, it was quite touching seeing Ian beg for mercy – he may have met his match."

"How long have they been cooped up together now?"

"Long enough Miles, but listen – as soon as we dock, we need to find the place where they're assembling the wagons I sent."

"They should have been assembled days ago when we were supposed to be here."

"I'm sure they're ready, Miles. I was told they do great work; but, like I told Joseph, we need to reassemble the ones we brought as soon as we dock."

The boat was a quarter of a mile from the West Port Landing. Miles looked at the very steep and uneven grade they would be ascending, scratched his head and said, "Hey – this wasn't like the map I saw!"

Suddenly the *Empire Lander's* bell rang and Travis heard a *TWEET* from the speaking tube. "Travis, is that bell what I think it is?"

"That's right Mr. Seagraves. We are here!"

"None too soon, Travis. We're running on our last cord of wood."

On the main deck, Nate and Jacobus heard the bell and walked toward the bow to see the landing.

The women and children who were still packing came out of their rooms on the boiler deck yelling, "We're here! We're here!"

Several crewmen turned to face Travis up in the pilothouse. They clapped as Travis rang the bell again and yelled down at them through his open window facing the bow "Alright, men! You did it!"

Then, a lone rifle shot unexpectedly echoed throughout the river valley. Everyone looked around to see what had happened. The crewmen on the starboard side of the main deck looked up toward the back side of pilothouse and saw Ian with his rifle. A waft of smoke dissipated above his head. The only sound on the boat now was the paddle wheel clapping against the water at the stern. Other passengers on the boiler deck had leaned out over the rail and were trying to look back up to the captain's quarters to see what had happened. Everyone, that could see Ian, stared at him in silence.

Ian sheepishly looked down, and while still holding his rifle, shrugged and said, "What? I got excited too!"

Will shook his head as the *Empire Lander* approached the dock. "It's never boring with him, is it?"

Miles said, "Never mind Ian. Is that landing all there is? It's no more than a few houses and shacks."

"It's only the landing, Miles. That bedrock ledge at the water acts as a natural boat dock. The outfitters are up past that bluff, but there are some people that are supposedly able to help us down here, too."

"How far south over that bluff?"

"Oh, a few miles up that gorge between the rocks."

"How do we get everything up there?"

Will rubbed his left hand over his mouth then pointed at several Indians with donkey carts approaching the landing. "Maybe, that's what we use?"

Miles looked down at the deck and muttered "If donkey carts and our paltry few wagons are all we have to get up that mountain – then it'll just have to do, I guess."

"Will pointed up to the gorge. "Mountain? Oh wait, Miles, look! Your little world isn't coming to an end today after all."

Miles looked up again and saw men leading oxen in front of several empty wagons toward them and said,

"Yeah, I guess we'll be okay, but this still isn't going to be cheap, is it?"

Will took in a deep breath. "Listen to you! First it's not possible. Then it *is* possible – but it's going to cost money."

"Will, I'm just saying…"

"This is why you're not married! Who besides *me* would put up with you?"

Miles raised his voice. "Now it's, *the marrying man* giving *me* advice!"

"Hey – I've had plenty of girlfriends – and I mean *plenty*…schnozzle!"

"Go ahead and get it out of your system, Will. I'm sure there's *some* woman out there that will have you."

Nate quickly walked to them and said. "Gentlemen – I'm using that word loosely right now. Check yourselves. This boat is not that large."

Will and Miles slowly turned to look over their shoulders and saw several women and children from the other party that had been traveling with them. They were all gathered on the boiler deck, right above them, preparing to disembark. The women were frowning and had their hands placed over their children's ears.

Will smiled and waved. They did not return the gesture. Then he looked down and softly said, "Miles, sometimes you bring out the worst in me."

"Miles frowned and whispered, "Shit, Will – we've got to get off this boat."

"Yep – we need to get everyone aboard those wagons and donkey carts – then figure out how to get the wagons we have up that gorge."

"What about our horses?"

"I don't know how you feel about Chipper, but I'm not whipping Lucky up that rocky gorge pulling a stupid wagon."

"You're right. I'll talk to those guys coming down with the oxen. I bet they'll know something."

Will sighed and pointed to an open area by the river. "You know what? This process may take a day or so. We might need to make camp over there for the night because when we leave this landing we're not coming back."

"No! We need to camp way over there next to the rocks with those kids."

"That's right! Damn it – I almost forgot – those little kids need to be as far away from the water as they can get. I'll talk to Joseph and Clyde about the camp and you find out how we get cattle down here for our wagons."

The stopping bell sounded. The Empire Lander slowly moved to the dock where Jason Winship and the rest of the crew tied the boat and positioned the gangplanks. Miles was the first off the boat. Nate had been holding Samson and finally let him go. He ran off the boat like a shot and urinated in various spots, howling all the while.

Will patted Nate on the back. "I thought we were going to be the happiest creatures to get off this boat, but I was obviously wrong. I've never seen a happier doggie, Nate."

Nate laughed. "I know it – new smells everywhere!"

In another area past the landing, up the gorge and over four miles to the south, a man in his late twenties moved a partially assembled wagon through the back doors of a warehouse. After he closed the warehouse doors, he shouted, "Monsieur Chapeau, what about the letter?"

Henri Chapeau was in his early sixties with a full head of thick gray hair that sharply contrasted his dark eyebrows and mustache. He looked through his wire rimmed glasses at the young man. "We don't know anything yet – so we have nothing to say. N'est-ce Pas?"

"But they should have been here days ago."

"Patience, Maurice – they could have hit a snag like the others," said the spectacled Frenchman.

"How will we know him if he enters?"

"I will know him."

"What happens when–?"

"Trust me Maurice – be ready – tell Reynard to be ready."

Will and Joseph carried the last trunk off the gangplank and saw Miles visiting with the other group that had been traveling with them on the *Empire Lander*. They were all milling around several wagons and donkey carts that had come down from West Port.

"Well, Miles what'd you find out?"

"The oxen drivers said our wagons *were* going to be down here, but they ran out of room in those little warehouses over there, so they're up in West Port at a blacksmith and wagon maker's shop. The drivers said they'll take these people up to West Port now, and others will come back in the morning with the oxen I bought."

"Miles, you keep saying *oxen* as if you were Sir Walter Raleigh stepping off the boat from England. You and I both know they're just steers – now run back over there and get us something to cook over the fire tonight."

"What?"

"You heard me, Miles – get with it – we'll be making camp and putting our wagons back together – now go!"

"*Errand boy* here is going to cost you, Will."

"Say what you want *Tree Stem* – I'm not asking you to go forage for wood – although you've proven to be good at that – just get us something to eat!"

Miles turned away saying, "Whatever, Will" Then, he intentionally kicked a rock which caused him to hobble a little as he walked back to the warehouses at the landing.

Will grinned and turned to look at Ian. "That looked a little painful didn't it? So – anyway, why don't you crack open a bottle of whisky and find our fiddler?"

Nate saw Miles limping away and said to Will, "You and Ian created a different person back there in the woods. He's going to get you back if you keep running him like that."

Will chuckled. "Right...Tree Stem, the killer! I'm quaking in my boots. Guess what, Nate? I don't care! We're finally off that damned boat, and we made it to West Port landing alive."

The next morning, Will awoke to the sounds of moaning. He slowly opened one eye and saw Ian rolling over on his side in a vain attempt to be comfortable on the hard ground. Will gradually sat up to see the camp fire was only smoldering now. He rubbed his head and thought, *It's freezing out here,* then said, "Damn it, Ian, no more of your cheap liquor."

Ian turned over and pulled his blanket over his head.

Miles was already awake, so he walked to Will, leaned over and whispered, "We're not sleeping with the animals anymore. Watch your mouth."

Will looked around the camp fires and saw Caleb, Katherine and Sammy sleeping in blankets next to their parents. "Okay Miles, thanks. What time is it?"

"Eight thirty."

"We haven't slept that long in weeks."

"Guess we needed it, Will. It's a lot more peaceful here than the boat. I'll talk to Clyde. We'll pack up and load the wagons."

Will pointed to the gorge. "Well you better hurry because here they come."

"What?"

"Look."

Miles saw several of the local Indians approaching them in donkey carts. They were followed by teams of oxen driven by several men with whips; and, behind them were empty wagons pulled by more oxen. Miles smiled and said, "Yes Will, they've come early."

"I'll say – it's the cavalry! We're saved. By the way Miles, that's a lot of animals. How much did all that cost you? Like you said in your little tantrum on the boat – they're the only game in town. I bet it wasn't cheap."

Miles turned to look at the oxen teams. "It was...uh...Wait! I've got to talk to their foreman, real quick. I'll be right back." Then, Miles jogged away. All the others took down tents and packed the camp. Will pitched in and helped most everyone including Miles since he had not returned. A half hour passed before he saw Miles walking back with a smile on his face, so he asked, "Why are you so happy?"

"Anytime I see that you doing all the work, it makes me happy. All I had to do was pay for everything we needed to get everyone up that hill and beyond!"

"Well, enjoy yourself some more and help us with what little is left." Within the hour, the trunks were on the wagons, and they were being pulled by all the oxen Miles arranged. Shortly after they started the slow painstaking ascent up the rocky gorge, Miles saw Will had stopped to the left of the procession of wagons. As Miles approached on Chipper, he said, "You've relinquished your leadership position up front I see."

"Yeah, I got to thinking and wanted to come back here and thank you for everything, Miles. After all your hemming and hawing, it looks to me like you've finally warmed up to this trip. Besides I've never driven cattle pulling heavy wagons up a hill like that!"

"Well, you'll be an old pro at it by the time we get to

California."

The wind blew harder. Will pulled up the collar on his light jacket – raised one hand from Lucky's reins and gestured at the passage up the steep hill. "Miles – all kidding aside – look at the line of beautiful wagons, carts, people and horses going up that slope and how the drivers whip the hell out those cattle pulling the wagons!"

"I know, Will. Look all the rocks those drivers have to get around, too. This isn't going to happen very fast."

"Even though our group isn't really that many people, it looks like they stretch almost a quarter of a mile straight up that hill. What a parade! Really top notch, Miles – my compliments for arranging it. How much did all this cost?"

"Don't ask...the guy said he was making me a special deal."

Will laughed and sat back in Lucky's saddle. "What'd he say? For *just* you, it'll be twice the price. Something like that, right?"

Miles slowly pulled back on Chipper's reins. Will and Lucky were now a few steps ahead of him. "Yes. I thought their price was way too high so I got them to come down a little, but it really doesn't matter."

Will said authoritatively, "Of course it matters, Miles. Money is *still* money, and you should always be careful how you spend it." Then Will sat tall in his saddle and pulled the front of his hat down slightly with his right hand. After that, he took Lucky's reins in his left hand and slowly brought his right hand down to rest on his thigh as he rode.

"It doesn't matter because it wasn't my money."

Will's smile and posture suddenly disappeared before he pulled back on Lucky's reins. "What! You didn't!"

"Yep – better watch where you leave your money belt."

Will was even with Miles now. His face turned red as he shouted. "You *un*believable little…"

"Cuss all you want – the kids are way up there and can't here you back here."

"Damn you, Miles!"

"You're going to hell, Will, if you keep talking like that."

"You're thieving my money belt, and *I'm* going to hell?"

"You insulted me in front of everyone back there on the boat."

"Me?"

"Yeah – then you pissed me off, ordering me around ever since we got here too. But I must say, spending *that* much of your money made me feel a lot better."

"You've lost your mind haven't you?"

"I see it this way. This trip was your idea. You simply made an indirect purchase to spare the horses – that's all."

Lucky slowed as Will shook his head. "Why don't you either ride up ahead or go back and get on the next boat to St. Louis?"

"Looks like I hit a nerve."

"Goddamn you, Miles. How much was it?"

"You're going to hell, Will."

At the front of the procession, Gretchen, Elizabeth, Abigail and Sarah were riding on one wagon with all the children. Sarah pointed behind them to her right. "Elizabeth, look behind you at those houses that overlook the bluff!"

"Oh my, what a view they have of the river valley."

Gretchen turned back to one of the men and asked. "Sir, who owns those houses back there?"

Before he could answer though, the burly driver saw one of the oxen team stop so he lashed the whip on his backside. "I don't know – I'm new here, but I think they belong to the French families who've been around here for a long time."

Will finally made his way back to the front of the wagons after hours of slowly riding up the gorge. He pointed to various houses and structures in front of them. "That's got to be West Port up ahead. Finally, we can stock up on supplies now for the next leg. Pass the word to the back that we see it."

Slowly the procession of wagons, oxen, donkey carts and horses followed by all those from Scott County came upon West Port Road and Pennsylvania Avenue. Travelers, traders, Indians, ruffians and charlatans were all gathered at this intersection. Men and women were walking to and from a two-story outfitting store built of logs. Will pulled Lucky's reins and pointed past what appeared to be a public well and yelled, "Fight!"

A crowd had gathered around two men who were arguing. Then the larger man with a beard pushed the smaller one. The crowd immediately began shouting for the person they wanted to win. The smaller man responded by charging the bearded man and jumping into the air with his right arm swinging toward the larger man's face.

Ian looked back at Will. "Look how fast the little guy is!"

The bearded man, however, sidestepped the flying blow, and the smaller man simply completed his arc in the air and hit the ground hard injuring his right shoulder.

Will's face grimaced as the smaller man squirmed on the ground screaming in pain. "Yep – it's everything we've heard about frontier towns, Ian."

Ian kept looking around at the crowd. "You're right,

some of these people are minding their own business, but I don't like the way some of them look at Nate and Abigail."

"I don't care, Ian. We go where we want. If others don't like it, then that's too damn bad. We will shop with pistols at our side if we have to, but right now I'm going to that wagon house up the street on Pennsylvania. Also, this is against my better judgment, but please take my money belt and help some of our people."

"Will, you're trusting me with the money belt?"

"I know there's a decent person in you somewhere, Ian. Don't disappoint me. I'm just going to see if we have wagons ready yet or not."

"Okay Will, I promise I won"t run away with your money."

"Why do I not feel comforted? Look, I'll be back in a few minutes, Ian. This shouldn't take long. You have the lists."

"Will."

"What?"

"You did it. You got us here in one piece without getting yourself killed. I...uh...won't be taking the next boat back. Killing that gang on the Ohio River was the most fun I've ever had."

Will held out his hand to Ian and said, "Me too, you old sot. There's more coming. We need you, Ian. We only have one life, right?"

Ian took Dutch's reins and turned his head when he heard Nate and Jacobus riding toward them. Then he turned back, looked Will in the eye, smiled and said, "Right, but you're *still* an idiot and don't forget it!"

Jacobus rode Dutch to Will and said, "Congratulations, you've survived the trip. Where's Miles?"

"He's *way* back there Jacobus, but don't worry – word

that we've made it to West Port will eventually reach him. In the meantime, though, I think I'll grab that big overcoat of his out of the wagon. It's getting colder up here."

Nate said, "Will, have you caught your breath yet?"

"What do you mean?"

"Looks like the whirlwind stopped for a minute."

"No, it hasn't. That's why I need Miles' coat."

"It's not the weather, Big man. I have never felt so alive."

"I never thought I'd see both you and Ian gushing all over yourselves at the same time."

"I'm serious, Will. You won't believe what Abby told me a few minutes ago."

"What?"

"We are finally free."

Lucky walked in front of Dominick, but Will turned him back and said. "Sorry, Lucky's thrown his left front shoe – but hell, Nate – this trip's a big deal in all our lives and she's right. We're all in this together."

"You might also heed Jacobus' words, Will. When I was talking to him about my doubts in this journey, he told me something that gave me a good deal of comfort."

"Jacobus the horse trainer and philosopher. What great words of wisdom did he hit you with?"

He said *"Nate, you always take your skills with you when you move to a new land."*

Will laughed and said, "I wish I'd thought of that."

EPILOGUE

Will walked Lucky up the block northwest on Pennsylvania Avenue and came upon a larger wood framed structure with the sign *Smith & Wagon* displayed above the entry door. He dismounted, tied Lucky to a rail, and walked into what appeared to be a warehouse with a large assembly area of wagons in differing stages of construction. The latest stage was a wagon without its tongue near two double doors that lead outside. To the right of the almost finished wagon, was an older man behind a counter with dark eyebrows and moustache, which stood in direct contrast to his full head of light gray hair. As Will entered the work area, the man raised a pair of wire-rimmed glasses to his face and asked, "May I help you?" in a heavy French accent.

"Yes, I'm Will Richards. I'm looking for the wagons I sent here some time ago."

The older man moved to a ledger. He felt his heart beat faster, so he subtlety took several slow deliberate breaths. "Let me check, Monsieur Richards. We receive a great many orders these days."

Will walked to the wagon nearest completion by the door and stated, "This wagon seems to be the type we ordered. It has the free turning wheels in front, and it's not too big."

The Frenchman ran his fingers down the ledger "Oui! William Richards from Kentucky – how may I help you?"

"Like I said, I'm looking for wagons I sent to you several weeks ago. Do you have them?"

The gray-haired man ran his finger down the ledger. "One second, Monsieur Richards...ah yes! Here it is." Then the Frenchman rang a small bell that was under the counter and walked toward the double doors. "Follow me Monsieur – they are back here." Will thought, *Why did he have to ring a bell?* and followed the Frenchman through the double doors. He saw many assembled wagons outside before he felt a sudden intense pain to the back of his head, then everything went black.

To be continued...